W9-DCG-293

GOOD NEWS FOR JILL!

Jill sank onto the couch, laughing. Her mother walked into the room, drying her hands on a dish towel.

"What's all the commotion?" she asked.

"Mom!" Jill said. "Fiona Bartlet isn't going to be an alternate on the Olympic team!"

Mrs. Wong's brown eyes grew wide.

The telephone rang.

"I'll get it!" Jill cried.

She jumped over the back of the couch and ran for the wall phone in the kitchen.

"Hello?" she said breathlessly.

"May I please speak to Jill Wong?" said a woman's voice.

"This is her. I mean she!" Jill said. "I mean, this is Jill!"

The woman on the other end chuckled.

"Jill, this is Kate Vandervleet from the United States Figure Skating Association. The Olympic Committee has an important question for you. We'd like to know if you—"

"Yes!" Jill shouted. "I do!"

Mrs. Vandervleet paused. "So I take it you'll be an alternate on the U.S. Figure Skating Team?"

"Yes!" Jill said. "Sorry. I'm a little excited."

"I understand, Jill. We'll be express mailing you some important forms. And I'll be in touch again very soon. But right now, I'm sure you'd like to tell your family."

"Thanks!" Jill hung up the phone. Randi and their mother were standing right behind her.

"Are you going to the Olympics?" Mrs. Wong asked.

Jill nodded.

"I'm just an alternate," she said. "But I'm going."

Gold Medal Dreams #3

CHANCE OF A LIFETIME

Melissa Lowell

Created by Parachute Press, Inc.

A SKYLARK BOOK

NEW YORK • TORONTO • LONDON • SYDNEY • AUCKLAND

12002
$9.84

With special thanks to Darlene Parent, director
of the Sky Rink Skating School, New York City,
and choreographer of Tori's skating routines
RL 5.2, 009–012

CHANCE OF A LIFETIME
A Skylark Book / February 1998

Skylark Books is a registered trademark of Bantam Books,
a division of Bantam Doubleday Dell Publishing Group, Inc.
Registered in U.S. Patent and Trademark Office and elsewhere.

ISBN 0-553-48527-X

Published simultaneously in the United States and Canada

1
Tori and Jill

Tori blinked.

Where am I? she thought.

She squeezed her eyes shut and opened them again. The swirling colors slowly swam into focus and turned into a circle of faces looking down at her. There was her mom. And her skating coach, Dan Trapp. And her good friend Jill Wong.

Oh, no! With a sinking feeling Tori realized that she was lying on the floor—in front of the biggest audience ever to squeeze into the Philadelphia Ice Arena.

She had just finished the best figure-skating routine of her life. In the U.S. Figure Skating Championships. Her scores had been incredible. She'd even received two perfect sixes. And then she had fainted.

"Tori? Tori? Can you hear me?" Corinne Carsen asked.

"Yes, Mom," Tori said quietly. Her voice felt weak. Her mother pulled Tori's head onto her lap.

Tori tried to sit up. Dan reached over and put a hand on her shoulder. "Don't move," he said. "An ambulance is coming."

"An ambulance?" Tori repeated. "I don't need an ambulance." She brushed Dan's hand away and struggled to sit up. A wave of dizziness hit her. Tori heard murmuring in the stands. Everyone was probably talking about her. How often did they see someone skate a bronze-medal-winning routine and then collapse?

"Are you hurt, sweetheart?" her mother asked.

"I don't think so." Tori shook her head.

"Let's get you to a seat," Mrs. Carsen said. She and Dan helped Tori stand. They walked her toward some plastic chairs in the front aisle.

Tori collapsed in a chair and leaned over. Blood rushed back into her head. After a minute, she felt much stronger. She sat up slowly.

A crowd was gathering around her. People pushed and shoved to get a better look. A film crew rushed over. Photographers snapped her picture. The electronic flashes blinded her. Tori felt her cheeks burn. She wished all these strangers would disappear!

"Jill? Will you please run and get Tori some cold water?" Dan asked.

Jill nodded and rushed off.

Two medical technicians pushed through the crowd. A burly man kneeled next to Tori and flipped open a plastic case. His partner pulled a blood-pressure cuff from her pocket and wrapped it around Tori's upper arm.

"How do you feel?" the first technician asked, studying Tori's face closely.

"I fainted, but I'm fine now," Tori said.

"Your blood pressure is normal," the other technician said.

The first technician shined a light in Tori's eyes.

"Did you hurt yourself when you fainted? Did you bump your head?" he asked.

"No," Tori said. "I think my mom caught me."

Her mother nodded. "My daughter has myotonic muscular dystrophy," Mrs. Carsen added. "She's fainted before."

Jill pushed back through the crowd. She thrust a paper cup of cold water toward Tori. "Here," she said. "Drink this down."

"Thanks, Jill," Tori said. She gulped the entire cup of water.

"We'll give you a full checkover at the hospital," the female technician said. "Sit tight and we'll get the stretcher."

"Mom?" Tori said, gripping Mrs. Carsen's hand. "Please! I don't want to go to the hospital. I can't leave here on a stretcher! I'm okay now."

Mrs. Carsen squeezed Tori's hand. "My husband is calling a local doctor who just saw Tori," she said. "He's going to meet us back at our hotel."

"Are you sure?" the female technician asked.

Mrs. Carsen nodded.

"Okay, then," the technician answered. "Let's clear out, Mike." Her partner nodded and snapped the medical case shut. He stood up.

A reporter suddenly shoved through the crowd and stopped right in front of Tori. He waved a microphone under her nose.

"Did you faint, Tori?" he shouted. "How do you feel?"

The technician named Mike pushed the reporter back.

"You're getting in the way," he snapped. "Stand back and give our patient some air."

Tori flashed Mike a grateful look. Just then Tori saw her stepfather rush to Mrs. Carsen's side. He was tucking his cell phone into his pocket.

"Dr. Mitchell is going to meet us at the hotel right away," Roger Arnold told her mother. "But the line out of the parking garage is a mile long. How do we get Tori back to the hotel?"

Mrs. Carsen gazed anxiously at the growing mob. Photographers, reporters, and camera crews were shoving toward them and shouting Tori's name.

Mrs. Carsen turned to Mike, who was pulling a red coat on over his white jumpsuit. She whispered in his ear. He grinned and nodded. Then he whispered in his partner's ear. She laughed. "It'll be our pleasure," she said to Mrs. Carsen.

A minute later, the two technicians pushed through the throng of people. Dan and Roger each held one of

Tori's arms. Mrs. Carsen and Jill walked right behind Tori. They moved quickly, in a tight clump.

The reporters caught up and pushed along behind, shouting questions. One stretched his arm past Jill and shoved his microphone under Tori's nose.

"Tori, can you go to the Olympics? How sick are you?"

Jill shoved his arm away and moved closer to Tori.

"Keep going," Jill told Tori. "Faster!"

"Tori! It's Marianne Magnan from *Time* magazine!" shouted a woman in a trenchcoat. "I was right, wasn't I? It's muscular dystrophy! You're sick, aren't you?"

Tori's group pushed out of the rink area into the huge lobby. Departing spectators crowded around.

"Move it, folks! Out of the way!" the technicians called.

"This is scary!" Tori told Roger. She felt panic rise in her throat as people pressed in.

"Don't talk to the reporters," Roger said, guiding her forward.

They reached the glass doors of the ice arena. Tori caught a glimpse of the parked ambulance. She looked at Roger. "Oh, no," she moaned. "Is that our ride?"

"Yes," Roger said. "Your mom's idea, of course."

The first technician pulled open the double doors of the big white ambulance. "Hop in, folks," he said. "You'll get the safest ride ever back to your hotel."

Tori ducked her head and climbed in. She couldn't believe it. She had just won a bronze medal at Nationals. That meant she qualified for the Olympics next month.

But everything was ruined.

She had fainted after her long program. And now she was being hauled away in an ambulance. It was like a bad dream.

How could the United States let her skate at the Olympics now? Why would they want *her*? Tori thought bitterly. She pushed back a sob. Nobody wanted a sick girl skating at the Olympics.

Especially a sick girl who was never going to get better.

Jill watched Tori climb into the ambulance. It roared off with its siren wailing. Jill turned and walked back through the lobby. She had to find her family.

"I knew it," Jill heard Marianne Magnan telling another reporter. "My source said it was myotonic muscular dystrophy."

The words sound so ugly, Jill thought. She stopped walking and listened to Marianne.

"I wonder what this does to her chances of skating at the Olympics next month," Marianne said. The other reporter murmured an answer that Jill couldn't hear. The two walked off.

What *will* it do to Tori's chances? Jill wondered. Would Tori skate for the U.S. at the Winter Olympics in Nagano, Japan?

With a stab of guilt, Jill realized that she was jealous of Tori! She was jealous of one of her closest friends. A friend with muscular dystrophy!

Despite the disease, Tori still *had* a chance to skate at the Olympics. Jill didn't. She had placed fifth at Nationals. A lousy fifth!

Jill felt tears come to her eyes. She swiped at them quickly. She was still wearing her pink skating costume. She didn't want to look like a bad sport in front of all the little kids and the reporters who were walking out of the arena.

I love Tori, she thought. If I could make her get better, I would. It's not about Tori, though. It's about me. It's about how I botched years of practice in just four minutes. Four minutes to skate my long program and fall on my triple loop. A jump I've done perfectly a thousand times!

Ludmila Petrova, her coach, had told Jill it didn't matter. "You will start again, and you'll skate at Nationals next year, no?" Ludmila said with her Russian accent.

Jill had nodded. But next year might as well be a million years away, she thought now. And there wouldn't be any Olympics. They wouldn't come again until 2002 in Salt Lake City.

Suddenly Jill spotted her mother's anxious face. Mr. Wong was right behind her, carrying Jill's three-year-old sister, Laurie, and herding her five other brothers and sisters.

"Mom!" Jill cried.

They hugged. Jill's family gathered around her.

"Fifth!" Mr. Wong said. "We're so proud of you!"

"Oh, Dad." Jill sighed.

Mrs. Wong pushed a stray piece of Jill's shiny black hair behind her ear. "We are *very* proud of you."

"Jill fell boom!" Laurie shrieked from her father's arms. "Boom!"

For a second the Wongs were all silent. Then the six-year-old twins, Mark and Michael, started to giggle. Jill couldn't help it. She had to smile.

"Well, like Ludmila says, there's always next year," she said. "And after I win Nationals next year, I can go on to the Worlds. That will be almost as exciting as the Olympics."

"That's the spirit," Mrs. Wong said. She frowned. "How's Tori?"

Jill shook her head. "I'm not sure, Mom. She fainted, you know? It was really scary. They took her away in an ambulance, but that was just to get her back to her hotel."

"That seems hopeful," Mr. Wong said. "That they didn't need to take her to the hospital, I mean."

"Yeah," Jill said. She felt bad about being jealous of Tori for going to the Olympics. Maybe she would talk it over with her mom later.

"Hey, Mom and Dad?" Jill said. "I can change out of my skating stuff at home. I'll just pick up my skate bag from the locker room and meet you back here. Then let's go straight home, okay?"

Mr. Wong nodded. "Are *you* okay, Jill? It's been a big day for you, too."

"I'll be fine," Jill said.

I'll be fine because I'll have lots of time to rest, she added to herself. She felt let down—as if she had nothing to look forward to.

In a week she had to leave her family to go back to the International Ice Academy in Colorado. She would be homesick all over again, missing her family back in Seneca Hills, Pennsylvania. It didn't help that she had the worst roommate in the world, Carla Benson.

And while the whole country was getting excited about the Winter Olympics, Jill would be back following her usual routine. Getting up at five every morning. Working on the same routine over and over. Falling on the ice, taking whirlpools to soothe her sore muscles, and falling again. Lifting weights until she wanted to scream. Doing ballet exercises until she thought her legs would fall off.

Jill rarely had moments when she asked herself if all the work she did for skating was worth it. But right now she was asking herself that very question.

She knew the answer, though. Skating was worth everything. That was why she felt so sad. Skating was everything to her, but she wasn't good enough to make it to the Olympics.

2
Tori

"**I** got them!" Natalia Cherkas cried.

She bounded into Tori's bedroom. She had a big stack of newspapers under her arm.

"I'm scared to look!" Tori said. She sat up in bed and glanced at her alarm clock. It was nine-thirty. Tori hardly ever slept this late. She stretched her arms over her head. They ached. Her whole body felt heavy.

Natalia flopped onto the lime green comforter next to Tori. She spread out the newspapers.

Tori knew the papers would be full of news about yesterday's U.S. Figure Skating Championships, called Nationals for short. It was the biggest amateur figure-skating competition in the country.

"Your mother had the man at the newsstand put every major paper aside," Natalia said with her heavy Russian accent. Natalia was the daughter of a Russian ambassador. She had come to live with Tori's family to be close to her father while he worked in Washington, D.C. Tori and Natalia were both members of Silver Blades, one of the best skating clubs in the country.

"Look for the *Philadelphia Enquirer*," Tori instructed. "That one probably has lots of coverage since Nationals were in Philadelphia."

As the girls flipped through the stack of papers, Tori thought about her third-place finish. It should have qualified her to skate at the Winter Olympics in Japan next month. But Tori was afraid that someone from the Olympic Committee was going to call and say they didn't want her. "We just can't take a chance," she imagined a voice saying over the telephone. "You're too sick. Sorry. Hope you understand."

Natalia held up a newspaper. "Here's the *Philadelphia Enquirer*," she said. She handed it to Tori.

Tori quickly unfolded it and scanned the front page. Almost every article was about Nationals. Splashed in the middle of the page were three photos of Tori.

The first one showed her landing the second triple-triple jump combination in her long program. The second one showed her lying on the ground with her head in her mother's lap. And the third one showed her climbing into the red-and-white ambulance in front of the Philadelphia Ice Arena.

"Oh, how embarrassing," Tori moaned. "They took a picture of me getting into the ambulance!"

"Well, look at it this way," Natalia said. "Usually

newspaper pictures show you from the front. This is a new angle for your fans!"

"Ha, ha," Tori said sarcastically. She tried not to think about how many people would see the photos.

"I came in third and I'm getting more coverage than Amber or Tracy Wilkins," Tori said. "It's ridiculous."

Tori's friend Amber Armstrong had won the gold medal at Nationals. Amber was also a member of Silver Blades.

Tracy Wilkins, a girl Tori knew only from seeing her at competitions, had come in second. And another girl she hardly knew at all, Fiona Bartlet, came in fourth. Then came Jill, who had been a member of Silver Blades before moving to Colorado to train at the Ice Academy. Tori winced just thinking about the results. She felt bad that Jill hadn't made the U.S. team.

Suddenly, Natalia gasped. She had been looking at the paper over Tori's shoulder.

"Look, Tori!" she cried, pointing to one of the articles. "Cara Hopkins is going to be on the U.S. Olympic Team!"

"But Cara didn't even skate at Nationals," Tori said. "That's not fair!"

Tori quickly read the article.

"It says the Olympic Committee asked Cara if she would skate in Amber's place," Tori said. "Cara's coach says her sprained ankle will be healed in time for the Olympics."

"But why isn't Amber going?" Natalia asked.

"Because Amber's too young," Tori explained. "Remember? They changed the rules. You have to be at least fifteen. She's only twelve."

"Then why doesn't the committee just pick the second-, third-, and fourth-place winners from Nationals to skate at the Olympics?" Natalia asked.

"I guess they try to pick the best skaters," Tori said. "And let's face it, Cara Hopkins is an amazing skater. She came in first at Nationals last year. And she was third at Worlds. She would've medaled at Nationals again this year if she'd been able to compete."

"So." Natalia squinted. "That means the U.S. Figure Skating Team has Cara. And it has Tracy Wilkins, because she came in second at Nationals. And it has you. And then the alternate who skates if one of you can't is Fiona Bartlet, because she came in fourth at Nationals."

Tori sighed. "This is pretty unusual. The Olympic Committee almost always just puts the top three skaters from Nationals on the team."

"Amber can't go, so they got someone else," Natalia pointed out. "It's not that big a deal. Amber is young. She'll get another chance."

"Don't you get it, Nat?" Tori asked.

"Get what?" Natalia said.

"If the Olympic Committee gets to pick who's best, why would they pick me?" Tori said. She could hear her voice rising. "I'm the girl with the stupid muscle disease. And even if the judges didn't see that *Time* article, they sure saw me faint!"

Natalia grabbed Tori's arm.

"So what? Dr. Mitchell said you would be okay. He even let us check out of the hotel last night and drive all the way home!"

"Oh, Natalia," Tori moaned. "Tell the Olympic Committee that! All they saw was me getting into an ambulance!"

The phone rang, making Tori jump. She and Natalia stared at each other. Tori held her breath and waited to see if her mother would pick up downstairs. She heard Mrs. Carsen's faint hello.

"That could be them," Tori said. Natalia nodded. She knew Tori was talking about the Olympic Committee.

Tori nervously toyed with the newspaper, folding its corner over and over. She looked up. Natalia was biting her lower lip.

"Veronica!" Mrs. Carsen called from downstairs. "It's for you."

Tori sighed and started looking through the rest of the newspapers. She heard Veronica pick up the phone in her room across the hall. Veronica was Roger's stepdaughter from his first marriage. She had moved in with the Carsens right before Roger married Mrs. Carsen.

"Evan! Hi!" Tori heard Veronica say. There was a long silence. Tori heard Veronica mumble a few words. Then Veronica's voice rose.

"No! Wait, Evan! I can explain!" Veronica cried.

There was another silence. Then Tori heard Veronica slam the phone down. A minute later, the sixteen-year-old was standing in the doorway of Tori's bedroom. Tori and Natalia glanced up.

"Thanks, Tori!" Veronica said. "For nothing!" She ran a hand through her short red hair.

"Why? What did I do?" Tori asked.

"You told Marianne Magnan, that stupid reporter from *Time* magazine, how old I am!" Veronica shrieked. "That's what!"

"She asked me how old you were!" Tori answered. "What was I supposed to do? Tell her I didn't know? Lie?"

"You were supposed to keep me out of it!" Veronica said. "That was Evan on the phone. He just read the article and found out I'm sixteen, not eighteen, like I told him."

"Oh," Tori said. "I'm sorry, Veronica."

"He broke up with me." Veronica sank onto the bed next to Tori and Natalia. She started sobbing.

"Veronica," Tori said, "I didn't know this would happen!"

Veronica had been dating Evan behind Roger's back. Evan was a sophomore in college. Veronica had met him a couple of months earlier at the Seneca Hills Junior College library. She had lied to him about her age—she knew he wouldn't date her if he found out how young she was.

The telephone rang again.

"That's probably Evan calling back now," Tori said. She patted Veronica's arm. "I bet it's him. Go get it."

Veronica looked up, her face hopeful.

"You think?" she said.

"Mom just picked up," Tori said. "She'll probably call you in a second."

The girls listened as Mrs. Carsen murmured on the phone downstairs. A minute later, they heard her bounding up the stairs.

"Tori!" Mrs. Carsen cried, as she rushed into Tori's bedroom. "Tori!" Her cheeks were flushed and her blue eyes were sparkling.

"That was the Olympic Committee!" Mrs. Carsen said breathlessly. "They said they would be proud to have you on the U.S. Figure Skating Team! You're going! You're going to the Olympics!"

3
Jill

"**Q**uiet, Randi!" Jill said.

Jill's eight-year-old sister put down her violin and glared at Jill.

"Mom said I could practice in here," Randi said.

It was a few days after Nationals. Jill had hardly left the house since then. She didn't even feel like hanging out with her friends from Silver Blades before she went back to school in Colorado.

"Tough luck, Randi," Jill said now. "This is the only room with a TV, and I'm trying to watch ESPN."

"Well, tough luck to you!" Randi cried. "I'm—"

"Shhh!" Jill said. The picture on the television had switched from the studio to a news conference. Jill pushed past Randi and turned up the volume. "Look! It's Fiona Bartlet!"

Jill and Randi stared at the set. Fiona Bartlet was

standing in front of a bank of microphones. She unfolded a piece of paper.

"I have been asked by the Olympic Committee to be an alternate on the U.S. Figure Skating Team," Fiona read. Cameras flashed in her face.

"I am most honored by the request. But I regret that I cannot say yes. I have already signed a contract with the Ice Magic Show. I will be skating on tour all spring."

Jill's mouth dropped open. "Can you believe it?" she murmured to Randi. "She's crazy! Why would she go on tour when she could go to the Olympics? Even if she would be just an alternate."

The reporters on TV went wild, shouting questions at Fiona. Her coach stepped onto the platform next to her. "We have no further comment," he called. The picture switched back to the studio.

Jill sat still, staring at the television. But she wasn't listening to the announcer. Her heart was pounding so hard, she couldn't hear anyway.

If Fiona wasn't going to be an alternate, that meant . . .

That meant . . .

Jill turned toward Randi. Suddenly she stood up and grabbed her little sister, hauling her to her feet.

"Randi!" Jill shrieked, laughing. She swung Randi in a circle.

"What?" Randi answered. "What? Jill! Put me down."

Jill sank onto the couch, laughing. Her mother

walked into the room, drying her hands on a dish towel.

"What's all the commotion?" she asked.

"Mom!" Jill said. "Fiona Bartlet isn't going to be an alternate on the Olympic team!"

Mrs. Wong's brown eyes grew wide.

The telephone rang.

"I'll get it!" Jill cried.

She jumped over the back of the couch and ran for the wall phone in the kitchen.

"Hello?" she said breathlessly.

"May I please speak to Jill Wong?" said a woman's voice.

"This is her. I mean she!" Jill said. "I mean, this is Jill!"

The woman on the other end chuckled.

"Jill, this is Kate Vandervleet from the United States Figure Skating Association. The Olympic Committee has an important question for you. We'd like to know if you—"

"Yes!" Jill shouted. "I do!"

Mrs. Vandervleet paused. "So I take it you'll be an alternate on the U.S. Figure Skating Team?"

"Yes!" Jill said. "Sorry. I'm a little excited."

"I understand, Jill. We'll be express mailing you some important forms. And I'll be in touch again very soon. But right now, I'm sure you'd like to tell your family."

"Thanks!" Jill hung up the phone. Randi and her mother were standing right behind her.

"Are you going to the Olympics?" Mrs. Wong asked. Jill nodded.

"I'm just an alternate," she said. "But I'm going."

Jill sniffled and wiped tears off her cheeks.

"I'll miss you guys," she said. "I wish you could come." She gave her father a last hug and stepped back.

The high-school band in the lobby of the Philadelphia airport started playing the national anthem. Jill was taking a charter flight with other Olympic athletes from the area. She had already greeted Tori, who was across the lobby with her own family. It had been three weeks since Jill learned she would be an alternate on the team.

Jill shouted to her father so he could hear her over the band's tinny music.

"Make sure you tape *all* the ice skating, Dad. You read the instructions for the VCR, right?"

"Instructions?" Mr. Wong said. "I'll just push all the buttons and hope for the best. Do I need to put a blank tape in first?" He grinned.

"Dad!" Jill cried.

"Don't worry, Jill," her eleven-year-old brother Henry said. "I'll be in charge of taping."

"Thank goodness," Jill said. "Don't even let Dad near the VCR."

Jill quickly kissed and hugged Henry and her five

other brothers and sisters. Then she gave her mother a hug.

"I'll see you soon, right, Mom?" Jill said.

"Right," Mrs. Wong answered. Jill's mother was going to Japan to keep Jill company. But Mr. Wong was staying home to take care of Jill's brothers and sisters. It would have been too expensive to fly the entire family overseas.

"My flight arrives in three days, Jill," Mrs. Wong said. "I'll call you as soon as I get to the hotel."

"Okay, Mom," Jill said. She glanced around the airport.

Athletes in official red-white-and-blue team jackets were milling around, saying good-bye to their families and friends.

Most of them would be competing, Jill realized. She wondered which ones were alternates like herself—athletes who would sit on the sidelines instead of being in the Winter Games.

Jill's mother pulled a small box out of her pocket.

"Here's something for good luck," she said. "We all picked it out." Mrs. Wong drew a silver skate out of the box. She pinned it on to Jill's official team jacket.

"Thanks, you guys," Jill said. She looked down at the shiny pin. She wasn't sure why, but it made her feel sad. They're giving me a good luck pin, but what do I need it for? she thought. It's not like I'm skating. I'm just going to watch.

Jill was afraid she was about to cry again. Even if she wasn't skating, she still wished her whole family could go with her. She wanted to share the experience with them.

The band stopped playing.

"Attention, Olympic athletes!" a woman's voice said over the loudspeaker. "It's time to board the plane through Gate 2! We're proud to serve you on this exciting day."

"Well, I'll see you all in about ten days," Jill said. "And I'll see you sooner, Mom."

Jill picked up her skate bag. It was too important to check onto the plane with her regular luggage. She couldn't take the chance that her custom-made skates would get lost. They were broken in perfectly. Jill would never be able to break in a new pair in time for the Olympics—*if* she was called upon to skate.

"Bye," Jill called.

She walked across the crowded lobby toward the gate. She bumped into a tall, pretty girl with long brown hair.

"Sorry," the girl said. She gave Jill a friendly smile.

"Hey! Cara!" Jill said excitedly. Her heart started pounding faster.

"Jill!" Cara Hopkins said. "How are you? I haven't seen you since we skated against each other—what?— two years ago?"

"Yeah." Jill nodded. The two girls smiled widely at each other.

"I am psyched to be on the same figure-skating team as you. Even if I am just an alternate," Jill added.

"Thanks," Cara said. "Hey, you're friends with Amber, right? Was she upset that she's too young to go to the Olympics?"

"A little," Jill said. "But she'll have another chance. And she can't really argue with Olympic rules."

"I guess not," Cara said.

"*I* was thinking of arguing with them, though," Jill added. "I mean, is it fair that the U.S. only gets to have three skaters competing? Couldn't they just make it a nice even number, like . . . four?" Jill laughed.

Cara grinned.

"Let's try to sit next to each other on the plane, okay?"

"Awesome," Jill said. She glanced around at the dozens of athletes lining up to get on the plane. They came in every shape and size, from huge and muscular to tiny and thin. Some held skis. Others had odd-shaped bags. Was that woman carrying a rifle bag? Jill wondered.

Jill spotted Tracy Wilkins, talking to an older man and woman who were probably her parents. Jill turned and saw Tori kissing her mother good-bye. That's the U.S. Ladies Figure Skating Team—all four of us, Jill thought, including herself as the alternate.

Tori rushed to Jill's side.

"Hi!" she said, gripping Jill's arm. "Isn't this great?" She looked past Jill. "Hi, Cara!"

"Hi, Tori," Cara said. "Jill and I are going to try to sit together. You'll sit with us, too, right? And we can ask Tracy to join us."

"Sounds good," Tori said. She waved her hand at the band and the throng of people who had come to see the athletes off. "This whole scene is like something you'd see on TV."

"Now everyone's going to see *all of us* on TV," Cara said.

"I should be so lucky!" Jill murmured. The minute the words slipped out, she wished she could take them back. It sounded as if she were bitter about being an alternate.

Cara and Tori stared at Jill for a second. Tori flashed her a sympathetic smile. But Cara just glanced out the window without saying anything.

What a dummy I am! Jill thought. It was true that she was just an alternate. But it was important for her to be a good sport about it.

"I can't wait until we all get to Nagano," Cara finally said.

"Me either," Tori agreed. "The sooner we get there, the sooner our team can win."

"Exactly," Cara said, putting her hand on Tori's shoulder. "But only one of us can win the gold medal."

"Sorry, Cara, but I happen to look really good in *gold*." Tori held up her thin gold necklace and giggled.

Jill laughed too. But inside, she was starting to feel miserable. Tori and Cara were having so much fun bantering about who would win the medal. Jill wouldn't even have a chance to compete.

Jill realized she was just as depressed now as she had been when she thought she wasn't going to the

Olympics at all. She had been thrilled to be picked as alternate, but that excitement had started to wear off in the past three weeks. And now, listening to Cara and Tori talk about skating in the Olympics, Jill realized that being an alternate wasn't enough anymore. She wanted to compete in the Olympics too! She wanted it more than she had ever wanted anything in her life.

"I feel like a human pretzel," Tori said. She stretched her arms. "We were squeezed into those tiny seats on the plane forever!"

Jill, Tori, Cara, Tracy, and the rest of the athletes were walking down the corridor of the Nagano train station.

Their plane had landed in Narita, near Tokyo, about three hours earlier. Then the athletes had boarded a Shinkansen bullet train. The trip took two and a half hours from Narita to Nagano.

"I can't believe how fast that train went," Jill said. "I felt like we were moving at the speed of light. And the scenery was *so* beautiful—"

"Oh, no!" Tori said, cutting her off. "Don't tell me all those reporters up there are waiting for us." She hoisted her skate bag higher on her shoulder. "There's twice as many as there were at Nationals!"

A huge cluster of men and women from the press were gathered at the end of the corridor.

Cara was nineteen and had been to several World Championships. She knew the routine.

"This is just the beginning," Cara warned. She ran her fingers through her long brown hair. "How do I look?" she asked Tori.

Before Tori could answer, reporters surrounded them.

"Tori! Can we get a quick interview?" a woman with a British accent asked, stepping forward.

"Cara, how was the flight?" A reporter from Cara's hometown newspaper took her arm, pulling her aside.

"Tracy! Tracy! Over here! *Sports Weekly* has some questions for you."

Jill stood alone, feeling left out. Didn't anyone want to interview her? She was only an alternate, but she was still one of America's top skaters. She wished that somebody would take a picture of her or ask her a question.

Jill watched as Tori easily fielded questions from the crowd of reporters. She gazed at Cara, who was laughing and entertaining two other reporters. A few yards away, Tracy was surrounded by reporters, too.

If this is how the next week is going to be, I might as well go home to Seneca Hills, Jill thought. She felt lonely and unwanted. She walked toward a drinking fountain.

"Excuse me." A reporter from the throng surrounding Tori stepped into her path. "Are you Jill Wong?"

Jill grinned. Finally! Somebody had noticed her! "Yes, I am," she told him.

"Great. You're one of Tori Carsen's best friends, right? I was wondering if you could tell me how she's doing." He held a microphone up to Jill's mouth.

Jill's happiness faded. All anyone wanted to know was how well Jill knew Tori. Jill shook her head. "You'll have to ask Tori," she said.

The reporter walked off without saying anything.

What a rude jerk, Jill thought. She stood there, waiting for Tori, Cara, and Tracy. She wished they would hurry up with their interviews. She wanted to get to the Olympic Village and dump all her stuff. And she wanted to be alone so she could feel sorry for herself in private!

Jill suddenly realized that the way competitors were treated at the Olympics was a lot different than the way alternates were treated. And Jill didn't think she liked the difference.

4
Tori

Tori wished the reporters would go away!

First they wanted to know how her trip was. Tori didn't want to tell them she had slept the whole way and was still exhausted.

Then the reporters started asking questions about her health.

She gritted her teeth and tried to smile. She couldn't let them know how tired she was. Or that her feet ached so badly she could hardly stand up. Even the muscles in her face hurt! But she had to appear strong. She didn't want the Olympic Committee to think choosing her to represent her country had been a mistake.

She glanced at Jill and saw her friend standing alone, looking lost.

"You'll have to excuse me now," Tori told the reporters standing around her. She walked to Jill's side. "Let's get out of here!" she said.

"I guess I should wait for Cara and Tracy," Jill said. "We're all taking the shuttle bus to the Olympic Village from here."

"Oh, okay," Tori said. For a minute she felt left out. She wasn't staying at the Olympic Village. Mrs. Carsen had talked Tori into staying with the family in a luxury hotel in Nagano. She had persuaded Tori that she'd sleep better in a hotel, and she would be protected from reporters.

"Well, Mom and Roger and everybody are picking me up here," Tori said. Mrs. Carsen, Roger, Natalia, and Veronica had all taken a commercial flight to Narita. It had landed at about the same time as the Olympic charter flight Tori had taken. Then the family had driven to Nagano in a rented car.

Tori said good-bye to Jill and headed toward the main exit in the lobby. It was packed with people rushing back and forth. The neon signs inside the lobby were written in Japanese.

Tori spotted Roger and her mother walking into the lobby, followed by Natalia and Veronica.

"Hello, sweetheart," her mother called. She rushed up and kissed Tori's cheek. "How was your flight?"

"Boring," Tori said. "I slept the whole way."

"You must be tired anyway," her mother said. "Let's find Ambassador Cherkas, and then we'll go straight to the hotel."

Tori sighed and nodded. She couldn't wait to get

back to the hotel. She was excited about being in Japan, but all she wanted to do right then was take a hot bath and climb under the covers.

Outside on the sidewalk, Tori heard a deep voice call Natalia's name. Tori turned and saw Natalia's father, Ambassador Cherkas. He was a tall, handsome man with graying black hair. Tori had met him months ago when he brought Natalia to the Carsens' house.

Standing beside Ambassador Cherkas was a petite girl in a fur hat and a long black coat. She looked almost exactly like Natalia! Tori recognized her as Natalia's sister, Jelena. There were pictures of her in Natalia's room back home. Jelena had decided to stay in Russia and live with her grandmother, instead of coming to the U.S. with Natalia. Jelena was a few years older than Natalia, but they were the same size.

"Papa!" Natalia hurried over and hugged her father tightly. "I am so glad to see you. Our flight was totally brutal."

"Totally brutal? I see you are still learning American slang," her father replied as he let her go. He smiled at her.

Tori watched as Natalia slowly turned to her older sister. She'd expected them to hug each other—they hadn't seen each other for months! But both girls stood there, eyeing one another tentatively.

"Jelena, I am very happy you are on the Russian Olympic Team," Natalia said in a stiff voice. "I started to write you a letter when I first heard the news—but I never finished it."

"Too bad," Jelena said. "I have not gotten a letter from you in a long time. It would have been nice to hear from you—especially about the Olympics."

"Sorry about that," Natalia said. But Tori didn't think she sounded sorry. Tori couldn't believe it. Natalia, one of the warmest, friendliest people in the world, was acting as if her sister were a total stranger. And Jelena was acting the same way. But why?

Tori knew that when the sisters were both still living in Russia, Natalia had beaten Jelena for the Russian junior championship. Was Jelena still holding that against Natalia? Or was it something else? Natalia hadn't been eligible to try out for the Olympics because she was a Russian citizen living in the U.S. Was she still upset because of that?

"You must be Tori," Jelena said.

"It's really great to meet you," Tori told her. "We love having Natalia stay with us. Maybe you could come to visit sometime, too."

"I do not know. I keep very busy with my skating," Jelena said.

"Oh. Well, think about it, anyway," Tori said. "I'm sure you could train at Silver Blades while you were visiting. We have a lot of fun in our skating club."

"So Natalia tells my father," Jelena said. "As you heard, she has not written to me much lately."

"I said I was sorry, Jelena. I've been busy," Natalia said.

"She's a terrible correspondent," Mr. Cherkas said, putting his arm around Natalia's shoulder. "Of course, it's easier for us, both being in the States. When she doesn't write, I call her on the telephone and bother her."

"You don't *bother* me, Papa," Natalia said, playfully hitting his arm. "Except if I am watching my favorite TV show."

"Well, shall we get going? I would like to get to the hotel and relax a bit," Jelena said. She and her father were staying at the same hotel as Tori and her family.

"Good idea," Ambassador Cherkas agreed. "The taxi line is right over there." He pointed to a line of waiting cars. "And you have a rented car, I believe?" he said to Roger. "For the seven of us, two cars should be enough."

Roger nodded.

"Hey, I have an idea," Tori said to Jelena. "Why don't you and Natalia and I go to the sauna room when we get to the hotel?"

"No, thank you," Jelena said, brushing a wisp of her brown hair out of her eyes and curling it behind her ear. "I have other things to do."

"Well, maybe later we can all get together," Tori suggested.

"Maybe," Jelena said. They all walked toward the cabs.

Tori got into a cab with Jelena and Natalia and Veronica. Her mother and Roger would drive the ambassador in their rented car.

Wow, Tori thought as the taxi pulled away. It was cold outside—but even colder inside, with two sisters who barely spoke to each other!

Tori gazed up at the luxury hotel as she got out of the cab fifteen minutes later. "It must be thirty stories high!"

"We'll have a great view of the mountains," Natalia said.

"The mountains—and everything else in Japan!" Tori said as they walked into the hotel. "We can probably see Seneca Hills from up there."

Tori watched as Jelena and Ambassador Cherkas checked in at the front desk. They were staying on the fifteenth floor. Tori and her family would be on the twenty-second.

"Natalia, can I ask you something?" Tori said.

"Sure. Go ahead," Natalia said, gazing around the lobby at the other guests.

"Don't take this wrong, because I'm really, really glad you're staying with us in our hotel suite. But, um, why aren't you staying with Jelena? Don't you miss her? I thought you guys were close."

Natalia shook her head. "We were close," she said. "But now . . ." Her voice drifted off.

"Now what?" Tori asked. "You don't get along anymore? Why?"

"To tell you the truth, Tori, I don't know why. Ever

since I left Russia, and Jelena stayed there with our grandmother, things haven't been the same."

"Don't you think you should find out?" Tori said. "Don't you want to work things out? I mean, if I had a sister, she'd be my best friend."

Natalia flashed Tori an annoyed look.

"Whoops," Tori said. "I'm sorry, Nat. It's none of my business."

"It's okay," Natalia said.

Tori squeezed her friend's hand as they stepped up to the desk in the hotel lobby. Mrs. Carsen was there, checking them in.

"Ah, Miss Tori Carsen," the clerk said. "I recognize you from the newspapers. Welcome to Nagano. We are thrilled to have you staying with us."

"Thanks," Tori said.

Mrs. Carsen signed the guest register. She waved to Roger and Veronica, who were sitting on a plush couch in the lobby. "We're checked in," she called. "Let's go."

Mrs. Carsen grabbed Tori's arm.

"You, young lady, are going to have a hot bath and go right to bed."

Tori saw that the clerk was staring at them. She flushed.

"Okay, Mom!" she whispered. "I was planning to do that, anyway! You don't have to treat me like a baby."

"Baby or not, that's what you're doing, Tori," Mrs. Carsen said firmly.

"Mom!" Tori said. She yanked her arm from her mother's grasp. "I said I would!"

She picked up her skate bag and strode toward the elevator. Her leg muscles twinged and her hand hurt as she gripped the bag.

Why does she have to be so bossy all the time? Tori thought angrily.

This was supposed to be the most incredible experience of her life! She was at the Olympics. She had worked hard to get here. She had done it against all the odds. But her mother still treated her like a baby! She still ran every aspect of Tori's life.

For the past month, her mother had dragged her from one specialist to another. Finally she had said she wouldn't go to any more doctors. She only wanted to see Dr. Wyckoff in Seneca Hills—the doctor who had diagnosed Tori's disease in the first place.

Tori liked Dr. Wyckoff. She never talked down to Tori or treated her like a child. She had given Tori lots of reading material about myotonic muscular dystrophy. Sometimes Tori was too depressed to read it. Other times, the books and pamphlets helped explain why she felt a certain way—why the muscles in her face, hands, and feet hurt so much. Or why she breathed so hard after she worked out.

Mrs. Carsen had finally agreed that Tori could see only Dr. Wyckoff. But she still bossed Dr. Wyckoff around, ordering her to give Tori all sorts of tests.

Tori tried to push the thoughts about her mother—and doctors and muscular dystrophy—out of her mind. Right now, she just wanted to be happy. She wanted to enjoy being in Japan, on the brink of competing in the Olympics. It would be a once-in-a-lifetime experience.

Once in a lifetime.

That was for sure, Tori thought. Her body hurt so much. And she felt so tired. This would be her last chance to skate at the Olympics. She was sure of it.

She wondered if it would be her last competition ever.

5
Jill

"**C**heck that out!" Cara said to Jill. She pointed out the shuttle bus window at a huge banner draped over the entrance to the Olympic Village. It had dozens of words painted on it, some of them in writing Jill had never seen before. She recognized several words.

"It says *welcome* in about a zillion languages," Cara added. "*Konnichiwa*—that's Japanese. *Bienvenue* is French. Oh, look, there's good old *Welcome* in English!"

The bus stopped and the girls grabbed their luggage and got out. They walked into a building with a hand-lettered sign that said CHECK IN HERE hanging above the door.

Inside, a Japanese woman was seated behind a large registration table. She had an OLYMPIC VILLAGE HOST button pinned to her blouse.

Jill stopped in front of the table.

"Hello," Jill said.

"Greetings." Cara bowed deeply.

The woman smiled and bowed from her seat. "May I have your names?"

"I'm Jill Wong. And this is Cara Hopkins," Jill said. "We're both on the U.S. Figure Skating Team."

"One moment please." She tapped into the computer on the table.

"Aha! Here you are," the woman announced. "You are going to be roommates."

"We are?" Jill grinned.

"All right!" Cara said. The girls gave each other a high five.

"You'll be in this building, upstairs on the third floor. Room 328. Here are your information packets. Read everything carefully," the woman said. "Especially important are the security concerns, and also regulations regarding visitors. Here are two keys and your building entrance codes. Good luck in the Olympics!"

"Thank you," Jill told her. She picked up her bags and headed for the elevator.

"It says here that the ice-skating arena is right in Nagano City. It's called the White Ring," Cara said. She was reading a sheet of paper from the information packet as the elevator rose. "The arena is six kilometers from the Olympic Village." She turned to Jill. "That's about four miles, isn't it?"

Jill nodded. "I guess they'll have buses for us."

The elevator stopped and the girls walked down the hall. They opened the door to their room.

"Hey, not bad," Cara said. She dropped her duffel onto the nearest bed. "It's not deluxe, but it's pretty nice. And look! We kind of have a view of the mountains."

Jill looked around the room. There were two single beds, two dressers, and one desk. A door in the far corner led to a bathroom—it wasn't fancy, but it had everything they needed, including a bathtub.

Jill sank onto the bed by the window and stretched her legs out. She was tired from the long trip.

"I think I'll take a nap," she said.

"Are you nuts?" Cara answered. "You don't have to save your energy to compete. You should go out. See Nagano!"

Jill sighed. "Yeah, I guess so." Suddenly, all her feelings about not being able to skate overwhelmed her.

"I'm kind of sad that I'm not competing," Jill admitted. "Don't get me wrong—I'm really, really glad to be here. But—"

"But you feel like you're missing out on the big show?" Cara asked.

Jill nodded.

"Hey, look at it this way," Cara said. "You'll probably skate in the next Olympics. This time around, all you have to do is have fun! You get all the excitement of the Olympics, and none of the pressure, which can be *enormous*. That reminds me, I'd better go find my coach."

Jill nodded. She snuggled down into the bed. She didn't have to meet her coach, Ludmila Petrova, until tomorrow.

"You sleep. I'll be back in an hour or so," Cara said. "We can go exploring and meet some of the other athletes on our floor."

"Good idea," Jill agreed.

"Um, I hate to sound really dumb. But what *is* curling?" Jill asked. She and Cara were hanging out with four girls from their floor.

They had already met people from all over the world—Sweden, Norway, Germany, France, Taiwan, Africa—and now they were talking with the foursome from Canada.

"You know what curling is, Jill," Cara said. "It's when you wrap your hair around hot, metal rollers."

"Oh, brother. We've heard every joke there is about curling," Beth, the team's captain, said. "Curling is . . . well, the easiest way to describe it is sort of bowling on ice."

One of the other girls, Marisa, said, "You have this forty-two-pound rock. And you slide it down the ice. You try to get it as close to the house as you can. The house is like the goal in hockey."

"Throwing rocks at houses? Sounds like fun." Cara smiled.

"Why don't you guys come to one of our matches? It's much easier to see it than it is to explain it. I could give you some guest tickets," Beth offered. "But I have to warn you—we're competing up in Karuizawa Town. That's about sixty-five miles from here."

"Oh. We might not have time, but we can try to make it," Cara said.

"I totally want to see you guys play. Why don't I know more about curling, though?" Jill asked.

"This is the first year it's been in the Olympics," another girl, Kate, explained. "A lot of people don't know about the sport yet—don't feel bad."

"Most people *do* know about another sport that's often confused with curling," Cara said in a deadpan voice. "Blow-drying."

The four curlers groaned. Cara and Jill giggled.

"We shouldn't laugh," Jill said. "Curling sounds like a great sport. And they're not making fun of our combination spins, and our triple flips—"

"Triple flip? Now *that* sounds like a hairstyle," Marisa said. The four curlers cracked up laughing. This time Jill and Cara groaned.

This is fun! Jill thought. Even if she was only an alternate, at least she was meeting some interesting people. Best of all, Jill was really getting to know Cara. She liked her a lot already. Jill could hardly believe they had only known each other for a day.

"Hey, do you guys want to get something to eat?"

Cara asked, glancing at her watch. "I think the cafeteria downstairs just opened for dinner."

"Sure, that'd be great," Beth said. Kate, Marisa, and the fourth girl, Marti, nodded.

The six girls went downstairs. The cafeteria was packed. Jill could hear snatches of conversations in different languages. A delicious smell was drifting over from the food line.

Jill and Cara grabbed trays and got in line.

"You're on the women's figure-skating team, right?" A woman standing in line in front of them, wearing the U.S. team colors, had turned around to face them. "I love watching you guys skate. I love skating, period."

"Thanks," Cara said. "What team are you on?"

"I'm competing in the biathlon," she said. "Hey, do you know Tori Carsen?"

"Sure," Jill said. "We're good friends."

"Lucky you! She's such a wonderful skater. I hope she wins the gold medal. I mean—not that you guys shouldn't. I want her to win just because of her health situation and all. Anyway, good luck!" She picked up a plate of food and moved down the line ahead of them.

"Everyone wants Tori to win," Cara said with a sigh. "The crowd's going to be totally behind her."

"Don't worry," Jill said. "I'm sure lots of people want you to win, too." She wanted to add, "At least you get a chance to compete."

Jill sighed. She really liked Cara. But she wondered if she should confide in her. Would Cara understand how she felt about being an alternate? Would anyone? Just then Cara grabbed a bowl of Jell-O from a dessert selection on the counter. She wiggled it under Jill's nose.

"When I gained ten extra pounds last summer, my thighs shook like that when I walked," Cara said. She wiggled her eyebrows up and down.

Jill laughed. "Cara! You're a nut! I am so glad we're roommates here. Even if you get to skate and I don't."

"Yeah. I bet being an alternate is kind of a bummer," Cara said.

Jill nodded, relieved that Cara understood.

"It is. A total bummer," Jill said. "I've always dreamed of skating at the Olympics. Now I'm here and all I can do is watch! I'd do anything to be on the team. *Anything*. Not skating is going to be the hardest thing I've ever done!"

6
Tori

"**M**y first practice. My first chance to see the ice!" Tori pressed the elevator button to hold the door open for her mother, Roger, Veronica, and Natalia. "This is so exciting."

"I wonder if the White Ring is as beautiful as everyone says," Roger commented, using the nickname for the sports stadium.

"Father said Jelena had her ice time this morning," Natalia said. "But I didn't ask him what the arena was like."

The doors closed and Tori felt a flutter in her stomach as the elevator dropped.

"Who cares about the White Ring?" Veronica said. "Did you see all those cool stores on the way from the train station?"

Tori laughed. "Actually, I was kind of busy, looking

at the mountains and all the other athletes walking around. And wondering where the ice arena was."

"Sports can really get in the way of shopping, can't they?" Veronica teased. "You've got to get your priorities straight, Tori."

"Veronica, too bad there aren't shopping olympics," Natalia said. "You'd win the gold for sure."

Everyone was chuckling as the elevator doors opened in the lobby. Mrs. Carsen suddenly gasped.

"What is it, Mom?" Tori followed her mother's gaze. A man with curly blond hair was standing at the desk. He was wearing a red wool ski sweater and faded blue jeans. He looked as if he spent lots of time outdoors—his skin was tanned golden brown.

"It's my father!" Tori cried. Mrs. Carsen put a hand on Tori's arm, but Tori brushed it off. She rushed forward. Then she stopped in front of him—she didn't know what to say. She had only seen her father once since she was a baby—for a short visit more than a year ago.

James Carsen smiled broadly. "Hello, Tori! It's good to see you again." Tori smiled shyly.

"Hi," she said. She gave him an awkward hug. "What are you doing here?"

"I came to watch you skate, of course! As soon as I heard you were on the Olympic team, I started making plans. I wasn't sure they'd work out. That's why I didn't contact you earlier."

"James. You're in Nagano," Mrs. Carsen said in an unfriendly tone as she walked toward them.

"Hello, Corinne," Mr. Carsen said stiffly. He turned to Roger. "You must be Roger Arnold, Corinne's new husband."

"Pleased to meet you," Roger said. The two men shook hands.

"This is my stepdaughter, Veronica." Roger put his hand on Veronica's shoulder. "And this is Natalia, a skater who's living with us now."

There was an uncomfortable silence while everyone stood around, staring at one another. Tori racked her brain to think of a way to make conversation.

"So, um, when did you get in?" Tori asked her father. "How long can you stay?"

"Until the closing ceremonies," Mr. Carsen said. "I'm planning to do some of my architectural design work right here, in the hotel, so—"

"You're staying *here*?" Mrs. Carsen asked.

He nodded. "I thought it would be convenient. They have home-office suites. I've got a fax machine, a copier, everything. This way I can see Tori skate and still do my work."

Tori heard her mother mutter something, but she couldn't make out the words.

"I realize you're going to be too busy to spend much time with me, but there are some things I wanted to say to you," Mr. Carsen told Tori. "The main thing I wanted to let you know is that I read a news story about your disease. I felt so terrible about the whole thing. I'm so sorry."

"Thanks," Tori said. She couldn't believe her mother hadn't written to tell him! They weren't in touch often, but Mrs. Carsen usually told her father about the important things in Tori's life. He must have been stunned to read about Tori's MD in a newspaper, Tori thought. It was sad that she and her father were so out of touch. Did it bother him too? she wondered.

Still, he was here now! Tori couldn't believe he had traveled all this way to watch her skate. Maybe this would be the start of a better relationship for the two of them, she thought. Maybe her father wanted to get to know her. She hoped so.

"It's time for Tori's first practice," Mrs. Carsen said. "If we don't get going right now, we might be late. Come on, guys."

Mr. Carsen walked beside Tori and Veronica. "Mind if I tag along?"

Tori shrugged. "I don't mind."

"I don't think that's such a good idea," Mrs. Carsen said. She stopped walking so abruptly that Mr. Carsen nearly crashed into her. "It might put added pressure on Tori. That's the last thing she needs right now."

"Mom, everyone else is coming," Tori pointed out. "What difference will it make if one more person is there?" She couldn't believe her mother was acting so mean. Her father was finally trying to act like a father. And her mother was ruining everything!

"Fine," Mrs. Carsen said, her mouth drawn into a tight line. "If you're coming, then let's get a move-on."

Tori sucked in her breath and gazed at the White Ring. It had a round, gently sloping roof and stainless-steel panels around the outside. It was beautiful.

She walked through the glass double doors. Reporters rushed over and started shouting questions at her.

"How do you feel?" one shouted.

"I'm feeling great!" Tori told the reporter. She didn't really feel great, but she forced herself to smile brightly.

"Are you ready for your short program?" another reporter asked, pushing closer to her.

"I can't wait," Tori said. "My short program is going to—"

"You're not afraid?" another reporter interrupted, before Tori could say anything more.

"Afraid?" Tori stopped dead in her tracks. "Of what? You mean, of landing all my jumps?"

"No—of fainting. Or falling again. Couldn't you really hurt yourself badly if you faint on the ice?" he continued.

Tori swallowed hard. She was so sick of reporters! All they cared about was getting a good story. Even if it meant being cruel.

"Tori's not afraid of anything," Veronica declared angrily, stepping forward. "So why don't you leave her alone?"

"The only thing she's afraid of is missing practice,"

Mrs. Carsen said. "Excuse us!" She shoved past the reporters, dragging Tori behind her.

"How does it feel to be diagnosed with such a serious disease on the brink of the Olympics?" a woman called out.

"Tori, what will you do after the Olympics?"

"What does life after skating mean for you?"

Natalia clapped her hands over Tori's ears. "Don't listen to them."

But it was too late. Tori had heard every word they said.

Nobody thought she'd make it through the Olympics. They all thought she was going to collapse, like a mechanical doll with worn-out batteries. And Tori was afraid. Afraid they might be right. She was still tired after the long flight to Japan. And her body felt heavier and more achy every day.

Mrs. Carsen stopped at the security checkpoint inside the arena. She pulled out the family's visitor badges and showed them to the guards.

"Excuse me, sir." One of the guards stepped in front of Mr. Carsen. "I need to see your badge."

"Oh, I didn't have time to get one yet," Tori's father said. "But this is my daughter. I'm here to watch her practice."

"Not today, you're not," the guard told him. "You need to go through a security clearance and get a badge."

"But he's my dad," Tori protested.

"Sorry. The same rules apply to everyone," the

guard said. "You can watch your daughter on the video monitor, right over there, while we check your identification and run a clearance."

Tori glanced at her mother. She was smiling triumphantly, as if it had been her idea to have security stop Mr. Carsen.

Mr. Carsen sighed. "All right. I understand the need for security, and I appreciate it." He patted Tori on the back. "Have a good practice, and I'll see you later."

"Serves him right," Mrs. Carsen muttered as they walked past the security desk. "Showing up at the last minute and expecting everything to be fine. Isn't that just like James."

"Mom, he's not *evil*," Tori said.

"Tori, please. I think I know him a little better than you do," Mrs. Carsen said.

"I'll be right back," Tori said. "I forgot to tell him something."

"Tori, your practice—" Mrs. Carsen said.

"I'll be right back," Tori cried.

"We'll be next to the rink," Mrs. Carsen shouted after her.

Tori raced past the checkpoint and found her father standing in front of the video monitor.

"Hi," Tori said. "I wanted to apologize for Mom. I know she's not being very nice. She just gets protective of me."

"I understand," Mr. Carsen said.

"So, what did you want to tell me?" Tori asked.

"Well, maybe it should wait until you have more time," Mr. Carsen said.

"Please tell me now," Tori said. "Otherwise I'll be wondering all day what it is."

"Can you sit down for a minute?" Mr. Carsen drew Tori over to a row of chairs along the wall.

"This sounds serious," Tori said slowly, settling herself in the chair. "Go ahead."

"This is going to come as a shock to you. And I don't want to upset you," Mr. Carsen said.

"Just tell me," Tori said quietly.

"Okay. Here goes. My mother had myotonic muscular dystrophy. As you know, some kinds of MD are passed on genetically—from one generation to another."

Tori had never paid much attention to where the disease came from. All she had thought about was that she couldn't get rid of it. Now her father was telling her that the disease ran in his side of the family.

"My mother had a very bad case. But before she got ill, she gave birth to me. And she passed it on to me. I have a very mild case. I never gave much thought to it. But then I heard that you'd been diagnosed. I felt horribly guilty. I don't know what I could have done, but—" His voice broke off. He sounded choked up.

"Wait a minute. Are you saying that I got muscular dystrophy from *you*?" Tori asked. "You knew you had this disease you could pass on to me—you knew before you even had me?"

The idea was incredible, she thought. Her father had never been part of her life. He had never even given her a birthday present! But he had given her the disease that was going to force her to give up skating. To give up every dream she had ever had.

"I just wanted to tell you in person," Mr. Carsen said. "My mother . . . she was confined to a wheelchair for most of her life. I didn't want to tell you that in a letter. But I also wanted to tell you what a wonderful woman my mother was. She never let the disease control how she lived. . . ."

Tori felt a rush of terror. Her father was still talking, but she wasn't listening. Instead, she was picturing his mother in a wheelchair . . . like the one she would be in soon.

"She became quite helpless," Mr. Carsen went on. "As a child, I had to help her do everything, but—"

"Stop it! You're scaring me," Tori said.

"But you need to know, Tori—"

"That's enough! I already know more than I want to. Why are you telling me all this?" Tori shrieked, standing up.

"I had to tell you in person," Mr. Carsen said, quickly getting to his feet.

"Why?" Tori screamed. "Why did you have to tell me at all? What good does it do? You gave me this disease. And now you want me to know how bad it's really going to get!"

"Please, Tori, don't shut me out. I can help!" Mr. Carsen said.

"You're right. You *can* help. You can stay out of my life from now on!" Tori said. "You should be good at that, since you've been doing it for the past fifteen years. Go back to your house and your new wife in Lake Placid. I don't want you to come watch me skate—not on Wednesday, not ever. I never want to see you again!"

Tori rushed past the security desk. She wiped the tears from her eyes and looked around. She had to get to the rink and find her mother. Mom was right all along, Tori thought. James Carsen, her father, was the biggest creep in the world.

7
Jill

"**Y**our triple axel is amazing," Jill told Cara as they sat down in the locker room after practice. "It's even higher than it looks on TV!"

"Can you imagine if Midori Ito were here to see you land that? She might be, you know," Jill added. Jill could just picture the famous Japanese skater sitting in the stands and watching. Midori Ito had been the first woman to land a triple axel in competition, nearly ten years earlier.

"I'm just glad I got all my jumps back after my sprained ankle," Cara said. She started untying her skate laces. "I wouldn't stand a chance without my jumps. Not with Jelena Cherkas around. She's such a good jumper, it's scary."

"I know," Jill sighed. "I hope she retires by the time I'm in the Olympics."

"Fat chance," Cara laughed. "She's only seventeen!"

"I can dream, can't I?" Jill asked. She wiped off her skates and tucked them carefully into her bag. She changed into blue jeans, a red sweater, and her winter boots. "I'm lucky I'm *not* competing, the way I was skating out there today."

"You looked fine," Cara said, slipping a team U.S.A. sweatshirt over her head.

"Fine isn't good enough." Jill bit her lip as she glanced across the locker room at her coach. Ludmila hadn't said anything, but Jill knew she was disappointed. "I was just so . . . so *nervous*. I wasn't even skating like myself."

"You do seem a little tense," Cara said, packing her skate bag. "Especially considering you're not even competing."

"Still, judges from all over the world are watching," Jill said.

"I guess I'm used to it, so I just ignore them. Judges are always watching. They're always standing around the boards, kind of like wallpaper," Cara said. "After a while they blend in."

Jill gave Cara an admiring look. Cara was so calm and collected. Jill wasn't used to hanging around with someone so mature.

"I'm still waiting for the judges to blend in," Jill finally said, tapping her boot against the floor. "I'm waiting for them to disappear altogether!"

Cara snapped her fingers. "I know a way to make them disappear."

"Oh, do you know magic?" Jill teased.

"No, but I know what I need to do when I'm getting stressed out. And that's to get away from the rink and do something fun," Cara declared, standing up. "Let's go check out Nagano City, the downtown area. It'll totally take our minds off skating."

"You mean, go on a tour?" Jill asked. "Instead of going right back to the Olympic Village?"

"A tour, a walk—whatever," Cara said. "We can grab an authentic Japanese meal, do some shopping . . ."

"That would be *great*," Jill said. "But I don't know if we should. I mean, are we allowed to just take off like that?"

"Why not?" Cara said. "Come on, Jill. Please? Pretty please?"

"Well . . . okay! Why not?" Jill said. "I've been dying to see what Nagano City is like!"

"All right!" Cara said. "We'll have a blast!"

Ludmila walked over to Jill. She had a slight frown on her face. "Jill? Did I hear something about going into the city?"

"Yes! I can't wait to check it out," Jill said, her brown eyes sparkling.

"There is a time to go sightseeing, and a time to stay in," Ludmila said gently. "You ought to spend the afternoon having a whirlpool, doing your stretching exercises, and relaxing. After the competition, *then* you can go on tours." She gave Jill's arm a pat.

"But we're leaving right after the competition,"

Cara said. "The long program isn't over until late Friday night, and we're going home on Sunday. One day doesn't give us nearly enough time to look around."

Ludmila glanced from Cara to Jill. "You will find the time, Jill. Now is not it," Ludmila said.

"But Ludmila—" Jill started.

"No buts. What if you end up having to compete, Jill? You have to be ready, just in case. And Cara *is* competing. You must not talk her into silly plans," Ludmila said.

"But it would only be for a couple of hours," Jill said. She glanced at her watch. "We could be back by two o'clock. What could possibly happen?"

"You know what, Jill? Ludmila is right. I guess I got carried away," Cara said. "Sorry. We'll do the whirlpool thing instead."

Jill stared at her. Cara had sounded so excited about seeing Nagano just a minute ago. Wasn't she as anxious to hang out in town as Jill was?

"Very good." Ludmila nodded. "Check in with me later, Jill. Please?"

"Of course," Jill told her. As soon as Ludmila was out of earshot, she turned to Cara. "What was that all about? I was waiting for you to back me up, but you changed your mind so fast I think I got whiplash."

Cara laughed. "It's an old trick I use with my coach. I let him think I go along with everything he says. But in reality? I only go along with him about half the time."

"You mean, you disobey his orders?" Jill asked, shocked.

"Orders? Nobody gives me orders. I'm an adult," Cara said. "I can make up my own mind about what's best for me. And it's worked so far." She removed her ponytail holder and shook out her chestnut-brown hair. She pulled a pink lipstick out of her pocket and put some on. "Come on. Let's go!"

Jill watched Cara head for the locker room door. Should she follow her? Ludmila would be furious if she discovered that Jill had disobeyed her orders. But Jill was in one of the most exciting places she'd ever been. She wanted to explore. Nothing bad was going to happen. And even if something did happen to Jill, it wouldn't matter. She was only an alternate.

"Well?" Cara called from the door. "What are you waiting for?"

Jill hurried over to her. "Nothing. Let's go!" As she pushed open the door, she wondered if they should ask Tori to come along. She paused.

"What? Did you forget something?" Cara asked.

"I was wondering if we should ask Tori to come with us," Jill said.

Cara frowned. "I hate to say this, Jill, but she didn't look very strong in practice today. She fell at least twice. And when she first walked into the arena, she was crying! She walked up to her mom and just started sobbing in her arms."

Jill frowned. "I didn't see that. I know she's got a lot

on her mind. I guess that's why I thought she should come with us. You know, to take her mind off things.''

"At this point, I don't know how she *could* take her mind off things,'' Cara said sadly. "It's probably better if Tori takes it easy, instead of running all over Nagano with us.''

"Yeah. You're probably right.'' Jill opened the door and walked out into the sunshine. "I'll call her when we get back. I hope she has a better practice tomorrow.''

"If she doesn't . . .'' Cara said slowly. "Well, if she doesn't, you know what that means.''

Jill was quiet as she followed Cara toward the shuttle bus stop. The bus ran from the skating rink to downtown Nagano.

"I'm not sure what you're getting at,'' Jill finally said. "Are you saying—''

"I'm saying that if Tori isn't well enough to skate, you will. You'll take her place,'' Cara pointed out.

Jill shook her head. She wanted to skate more than anything. But she didn't want Tori to get so sick that she couldn't skate! Still, it wasn't the first time Jill had thought about it. It was hard *not* to think about how sick Tori was.

What would happen if Jill had to step into her place? Would it ruin her friendship with Tori? Jill prayed that it wouldn't. But she knew that if Tori couldn't skate, she would have to.

"Too bad there aren't four spots on the team, like

you said the other day," Cara said, breaking into Jill's thoughts. She stepped onto the bus. It was filled with athletes, on their way to the city.

"That would be the perfect solution, wouldn't it?" Jill said. "They'd have to add a new medal, though. Gold, silver, bronze . . ."

"And brass. No, wait—copper," Cara joked.

"I'd settle for nickel. *This* time," Jill said. "I'd take anything, as long as it meant I was on the team!"

"I can't believe you'd never had sushi before," Cara said.

Jill followed Cara out of the small restaurant in downtown Nagano City. She gazed at the mountains as they walked back to the shuttle stop. People were sledding nearby on one of the foothills.

"That looks like fun," Jill said.

"You know what I've always wanted to try? The luge. I can't imagine anything more thrilling than bombing down that chute at sixty miles an hour, or however fast they go," Cara said.

"I can't imagine anything more *scary*," Jill said. "I'd have to keep my eyes closed the whole way. Then I wouldn't be able to see where I was going."

"Yeah, and you'd crash and burn!" Cara said with a laugh. "Maybe after our competition is over, we could give it a try. I think they give lessons."

"I'll stick to sledding. You should see the hills we

have back home in Pennsylvania. They're awesome," Jill said. "My whole family piles onto one of those really long toboggans—all my little brothers and sisters." She sighed, wishing her family were here with her right now.

"I've got an idea," Cara said. "Why don't we rent a sled from that guy over there and try out these hills?"

"Are you kidding?" Jill looked at the people flying down the steep hill, shrieking with laughter. "I don't think that's such a good idea. I mean, what if one of us got injured?"

"Oh, come on!" Cara pleaded. "Nothing is going to happen. We'll pretend it's the luge. Then we'll go home and soak in the whirlpool, just like your coach said."

"I don't know," Jill said.

"Come on, Jill!" Cara said. "When are you going to get the chance to go sledding in Japan again?"

"Well . . . okay." Jill nodded. She knew sledding was a crazy idea, but Cara was right. What could happen? Jill had never gotten hurt sledding. And she didn't know anyone else who had, either.

The girls hurried over to the booth. Jill pointed to the wooden sleds behind the man and held up one finger.

"Do you want to rent a sled?" the man asked.

"Oh—you speak English!" Jill laughed. "Sorry. Yes, we'd like to rent one of those."

"For an hour?" he asked.

"Actually . . ." Cara glanced at her watch. "We

don't have a lot of time. Could we have it for fifteen minutes? For a reduced price?''

"Here. No money necessary. Special price for athletes.'' He smiled at them and picked up a sled.

"Thanks,'' Jill and Cara said at the same time.

Jill grabbed the sled and dragged it behind her as she and Cara climbed the steep hill. At the top of the slope, Jill looked down. It was a long way to the bottom.

"This is crazy,'' Jill said. "Maybe this isn't such a good idea after all.''

"Oh, come on, you big baby,'' Cara said. She plunked down on the back of the sled and patted the front. "You steer,'' she told Jill.

Jill sat down and Cara grabbed her around the waist. "Let's do it!''

Jill pushed off, then held the rope on the front of the sled. She pulled it to the right as they started down the hill—slowly at first, and then quickly gathering speed. The sled hurtled down the hill, past sledders making their way back up to the top.

"Wheeee!'' Cara cried. "Go faster!''

Jill jerked the rope to the left to avoid another sled. Small snow crystals blew onto her face as the sled went faster and faster. She steered to the right to avoid a giant bump.

"Moguls!'' Jill cried. "Hold on tight!''

"What?'' Cara called back.

"Moguls,'' Jill turned around and screamed to Cara. "It's just like skiing—''

All of a sudden, the sled hit a large bump. It flew off the hill into the air.

"Nooo!" Jill cried.

The sled turned sideways in the air. Then it crashed down. The front end hit first and the back went flying into the air.

Jill catapulted off the sled, legs first. She heard Cara yell as she was pitched off.

Jill landed face down on the snow. She sat up, laughing, as she watched the empty sled run down to the bottom of the hill without them.

"That was fun! Let's do it again!" Jill called.

She looked at Cara, who was lying on the ground a few feet away. Her friend wasn't moving.

"Cara? Are you okay?" Jill asked. She scrambled to Cara's side. When she got closer, she saw that Cara's left leg was turned awkwardly underneath her.

"It's my—my ankle," Cara sobbed. She looked up at Jill. Disbelief covered her face. "I think it's broken!"

8
Jill

"Let me go develop these X rays." The doctor smiled at Cara as he pushed his black-framed glasses up the bridge of his nose. "I'll be right back." He walked out of the exam room.

Jill looked over at Cara. She was sitting on the exam table, her ankle propped on a bag of ice. The man renting sleds had found a cab to take them to the medical center at the Olympic Village. Jill had helped Cara limp inside.

Now Cara leaned forward and pressed the ankle with her fingertips.

"How does it feel?" Jill asked.

"How do you think it feels?" Cara said, not looking at her. "It *hurts*. Even more than the last time I injured it."

"I'm so sorry," Jill said. "I had no idea that

bump was there. I turned around to say something, and—"

"And steered us right into a bump," Cara muttered angrily.

Jill didn't know what to say.

There was a brief knock at the door, and the doctor walked back into the room. "Good news, Cara. Nothing's broken."

"Oh, good!" Cara said.

"That means we don't have to set it in a cast." The doctor smiled at Cara. "That was the good news. The bad news is that you've got a horrible sprain. I'll tape it up for you."

"Great. So I can still skate, right?" Cara asked.

"I'm sorry, Cara," the doctor said, shaking his head. "In fact, I wouldn't advise putting any weight on it at all for the next couple of weeks."

"But—that's impossible," Cara said. "I have to skate for the U.S. team this week."

"You can't skate, Cara," the doctor said. "You'll have to withdraw."

"No!" Cara cried. "I can't. There has to be a way to *fix* this. It's just a sprained ankle. People have skated with much worse injuries than that. Oksana Bauil skated with a slipped disk!"

"I'm sorry, Cara," the doctor said.

"You could put it in a splint—from now until the competition," Cara went on, ignoring the doctor. "And you could give me medicine to handle the pain—"

"Cara," the doctor cut her off. "Your ankle is severely sprained. You can alternate putting heat and ice on it. The swelling should go down in a few days. I'll give you some crutches. They'll help you get around for the next couple of weeks without putting any weight on your ankle." The doctor pushed the X rays into Cara's medical file.

Jill felt stunned. Cara couldn't skate! Did that mean Jill would?

Cara suddenly burst out crying, her body racked by sobs.

"I don't care what you say," she shouted. "I'm skating."

The doctor put his hand on Cara's arm. "I'm sorry. But competing won't be possible for you."

Cara shook off his hand. She rubbed her eyes with the sleeve of her sweatshirt.

"I'll be *fine*," Cara seethed. "It's twisted. That's all." She hopped off the table onto her good ankle. She put a tiny bit of weight on her bad ankle and winced.

Jill rushed forward to help her, but Cara waved her away.

"Take the crutches. You'll need them." The doctor opened the supply closet door and pulled out a pair of crutches. He handed them to Cara.

"I'll take them. But this isn't the end. I'll *skate*," Cara insisted.

Jill held the door open for Cara. "I can help you get back to our room," she offered.

"I'm not going back to our room," Cara said, swinging smoothly down the hall on her crutches.

"Where are you going?" Jill asked, scurrying to keep up.

"I'm calling my coach. He'll know what to do," Cara said. She stopped at the receptionist's desk. "Could I use the telephone, please?"

"Certainly," the young man at the desk replied. He handed the receiver to Cara.

Cara dialed a number. "Coach Bristol, it's me. I—I think I might have hurt my ankle again. Can you do me a favor? Can you get my skates and meet me at the rink?"

Jill couldn't believe her ears. Cara was going to try to skate now? But the doctor said Cara couldn't even walk. Their harmless sled ride had turned into a nightmare!

Cara hung up the phone and turned to Jill. "If you want to help, you could get me to the rink."

"Sure," Jill said. "But do you really think skating's a good idea? You're on crutches."

"It's not permanent," Cara said. She hobbled toward the front door and stood there, waiting for Jill to open it.

Jill walked toward her with a sinking feeling. She couldn't imagine how Cara would skate. And the last thing she wanted to do was watch her try.

"Here are your skates." Bill Bristol, a tall, thin man, shoved the skates into Cara's hands. She and Jill were sitting on a bench inside the Olympic rink. "I got a special clearance for us to be here, but we've only got ten minutes before the men's team needs the ice. Hurry and put them on." He sounded angry. "How did you manage to hurt your ankle again?"

"It was stupid. We were just . . . sledding, that's all." Cara's ankle was wrapped tightly in an ace bandage. The doctor had given her a big sock to wear over the bandage—her sneaker wouldn't fit. Jill could see that Cara's ankle was almost twice its normal size.

"Sledding? Are you kidding? What were you thinking?" the coach shouted, his face getting red. He bent down and took a closer look at Cara's ankle. "Can you put any weight on it?"

"Sure," Cara said, nodding.

Jill raised an eyebrow. That wasn't true at all! Cara could hardly touch her foot to the ground. She was obviously desperate to compete.

Jill had heard of top athletes playing through pain before, but she'd never seen anyone look as determined as Cara.

Cara put a skate on her right foot. Then she tried to pull the other skate over her left foot. She managed to get her toes halfway in before her foot got jammed. She tugged on the skate, trying to force it over the bandage.

"I don't know, Cara. Is that going to work?" Coach Bristol asked.

"It has to," Cara said. She grunted as she pulled the skate as far as it would go. Jill saw that Cara's hands were shaking as she tried to loosen the laces.

"Cara," Coach Bristol said slowly.

"I'll do it. Just wait!" Cara snapped. She yanked at the laces and pulled harder on the skate.

"It's no use, Cara. You can't even get your skate on," Coach Bristol said. "There's no way you can jump on that ankle."

"All I need to do is stretch it out," Cara said stubbornly.

"Your ankle looks worse than it did two months ago," her coach said. "Take off those skates before you hurt yourself more."

Cara yanked off her skates. She sat very still for a minute. Then she looked up at Jill, her jaw clenched and tears streaming down her face.

"How could you do this to me?" Cara moaned.

"Do this to you?" Jill repeated. "What do you mean?"

"This is all your fault! You did this on purpose, so that you could get onto the team. You said you'd do anything to skate in the Olympics. Well, I guess this proves it!"

"No, Cara!" Jill shook her head. "I'd never do something like that! I wasn't even sure we should have gone sledding in the first place, remember?"

Jill couldn't believe what was happening. Cara had been so friendly before. And now she was so angry. Angry at Jill!

"What's all the commotion?" a woman's voice suddenly asked.

Jill turned around. She was startled to see Kate

Vandervleet, the top official from the United States Figure Skating Association. Mrs. Vandervleet had visited Jill and her family in Seneca Hills shortly after Jill had been named as an alternate.

"I'm here to watch the men practice," Mrs. Vandervleet said. "But I'm a bit early. Wasn't your practice over hours ago?"

"It was, Kate," Coach Bristol said. "But Cara has a slight problem. She's just reinjured her bad ankle."

"Oh no!" Mrs. Vandervleet gasped. "How did that happen?"

"We were sledding," Cara began. "The sled flipped over. Now my ankle's sprained horribly—and it's all Jill's fault!"

"Jill's fault? I don't understand," Mrs. Vandervleet said.

"Jill was steering. She steered us right into a mogul so I'd fall off and hurt myself. She obviously wants to skate in my place," Cara said.

Mrs. Vandervleet turned to Jill.

"That's not true!" Jill cried. How could Cara think she'd ever do anything so horrible? "It was an accident. I didn't even want to *go* sledding."

"What are you talking about?" Cara interrupted. "You're the one who talked about what a great time you always had sledding with your family."

"Look, none of that matters now," Mrs. Vandervleet said. "We need to assess your injury, Cara."

Cara bit her lip. "What does that mean?"

"Can you skate? Will you be ready for the

short program on Wednesday?" Mrs. Vandervleet asked.

"She can't even get her skate on over the swelling," Coach Bristol said. He shook his head. "I'm afraid our Olympic dream is over, Cara."

"No!" Cara cried. "It isn't. It can't be."

"I know it's upsetting, Cara. We *all* believe in your skating. But if you can't skate, we need to put Jill on the team in your place," Mrs. Vandervleet said.

"She doesn't deserve to be on the team—not after what she did to me," Cara snarled.

"But Cara, it was an accident," Jill said. "I never meant for any of this to happen."

"All I know is that I'm sitting here with a sprained ankle. And you're on the team now," Cara snapped.

"I never planned this, Cara!" Jill said.

"Maybe you didn't." Coach Bristol stared at Jill angrily. "But do you realize that because of your carelessness, you've just given Cara an injury that will keep her out of the Olympics?"

"But it's not my fault. We were both sledding. We're both responsible. We hit a mogul—there was nothing I could do!" Jill protested.

"I'm so sorry, Cara. You're a wonderful skater, and we'll miss having you on the U.S. team," Mrs. Vandervleet said.

"Come on, Cara. I'll take you back to your room," Coach Bristol said.

"This isn't over," Cara said to Jill. She picked up her crutches. "Not by a long shot."

"Cara, how many times can I say that I'm sorry?" Jill was on the verge of tears herself.

Cara pulled her scarf tightly around her neck and leaned on her coach. "It doesn't matter how many times you say it. I'll *never* forgive you!"

9
Jill

"Oh, Tori," Jill cried as she walked into the Carsens' hotel suite that night. "Did you hear?"

Tori nodded and opened the door wide.

"It's so exciting!" Tori said. "It was on the Olympic news channel here! I can't believe you're skating!"

Tori pulled Jill into the room and gave her a quick hug. She stood back and eyed Jill. "What's wrong? Aren't you excited?"

Jill shook her head, and then nodded.

"Yes! No! I don't know what I am!" she said. "Did the news channel say what happened?"

"Just that Cara reinjured her bad ankle in a sledding accident," Tori said. "And you're skating in her place."

"I was with Cara on that sled. And I was steering

it," Jill said. "We hit a mogul. It was an accident. But Cara thinks I did it on purpose!"

The girls walked over to the couch in the living room and plunked down.

"Anyway, thanks for letting me come over," Jill continued. "Mom isn't getting here until tomorrow. And I just needed someone to talk to."

"That's what friends are for," Tori said. "And I'm sure the Olympic Committee and Mrs. Vandervleet know it was an accident, right?"

"I guess." Jill sighed. "If they didn't think it was an accident, I'm sure they wouldn't have put me on the team."

Jill idly picked up a magazine from the coffee table and then threw it back down.

"How's it going for you?" she asked Tori.

"I don't know. Worse?" Tori leaned back on the couch. "Jill, what's going on here? This is *supposed* to be the best time of our lives."

"I know," Jill said with a sigh. The girls sat there in silence for a moment.

"I'm glad I'm on the team. But I didn't want to get on it the way I did," Jill said. "And Cara! She's blaming me for ruining her life. I don't know how I'm going to skate, with her hating me so much."

"She'll get over it. It was an accident," Tori said.

"Tell Cara that. Before she reports me to the Japanese police for assault with a deadly sled," Jill said. She faced Tori. "So tell me about your day."

"Ugh. Do I have to?" Tori paused, biting her lip.

Jill watched Tori's face. It was turning red, the way it did when Tori was furious.

"My father said he had some news for me. At first, he acted all friendly. As if he was really concerned about me. Then he dropped the bombshell. He has muscular dystrophy. So did my grandmother. And that's why *I* have it—because of them!"

"What?" Jill asked, disbelieving.

"It's true. My father decided to show up after all these years so he could give me some really great news—right before the biggest skating competition of my life," Tori fumed. "Thanks, *Dad*. Thanks for ruining my life!"

Jill toyed with a pillow on the couch. "He sure picked a lousy time to show up."

"I know. He told me this story about how sick his mother got, and . . . it was horrible," Tori said. "It was scarier than anything the doctors have ever said to me." She groaned. "I hate him. I told him not to come watch me skate. I don't want him anywhere near me."

Veronica and Natalia walked into the living room.

"Is this a little Olympic athletes' party, or can anyone join in?" Veronica asked. She sat down in an armchair.

"This is a new part of training. It's called lounging," Natalia teased. She stopped smiling when she saw how miserable Tori and Jill looked. "Both you guys look terrible."

Jill moaned. "Cara Hopkins hurt her ankle while we

were sledding. She thinks I crashed the sled on purpose just to get on the team—and ruin her life.''

Veronica cleared her throat. "You and Tori have a lot in common, Jill," she said. "You ruined Cara's life and Tori ruined mine.''

"What are you talking about, Veronica?" Tori snapped.

"You told that reporter my real age, and Evan dumped me," Veronica said. "And now my life is ruined.''

"Oh, please!" Tori said. "I already told you, I didn't do it on purpose.''

"All I know is that one minute I was going out with the best-looking guy in Seneca Hills—make that the *only* good-looking guy in Seneca Hills—and then you opened your big mouth. And now I'm *not* going out with him.''

"Quit being a drama queen, Veronica," Tori said. "Evan was too old for you anyway.''

Jill sighed. Tori hadn't meant for Evan to break up with Veronica. But he had, and Veronica blamed Tori. Jill hadn't meant for Cara to sprain her ankle, either. But she had. And now she was blaming Jill. Maybe when things went wrong, people needed someone else to blame.

Jill felt even worse than she had before she got to Tori's hotel room. Cara hated her guts. Jill couldn't stop thinking about it. But she had to! She had to concentrate on the fact that, in two days, she would skate in front of the entire world!

Jill slowly opened her eyes the next morning. She glared at the buzzing travel alarm clock. How could it be seven o'clock already? The last thing she could remember was being wide awake at midnight . . . and still being awake at one . . . and then at two . . .

Cara had kept her up all night because she was watching television. Every time Jill asked Cara to turn down the volume, Cara said something about how she couldn't sleep because her ankle hurt too much.

Fine, Jill thought. Her ankle hurts, and now my head hurts! Jill always got a headache when she didn't get enough sleep. She swung her legs over the edge of the bed, knowing it was time to take a hot shower and get going. She needed to be at the rink in two hours for her final practice before the short program the next day.

Jill was on her way into the bathroom when she heard a loud moan. She turned around and saw Cara struggling to get out of bed. She had just put her left foot on the floor. Cara's ankle was still very swollen and had begun to turn purple.

"Can I do anything to help?" Jill asked, trying to sound cheerful.

"I think you've done enough already, don't you?" Cara sank back onto her bed and grimaced, rubbing her ankle.

"I'm sorry," Jill said. "I'm sorry we went into town

instead of sitting in a whirlpool. I'm sorry we went sledding. I'm sorry the sled flipped—"

"You're sorry *you* flipped it, you mean," Cara said.

"I didn't do it on purpose, and you know it," Jill said. She was starting to feel less sorry for Cara—and more angry with her!

"I'm not going to keep apologizing forever, Cara," Jill went on. "It was an accident, and I'm sorry about it. But I can't change what happened!"

"No kidding. Not that you'd change it, if you could," Cara said. "Because that would mean I was still on the team, and you were still an alternate."

Jill stared at Cara for a moment, trying to get control of her emotions. Why did Cara have to make her feel so guilty? Couldn't she just accept what happened and move on? "I'd be glad if you were still on the team. You know that. Nobody supported you more than I did. I was behind you, one hundred percent."

"Sure, Jill. That's why, ever since I met you, you kept talking about how you wished you were competing. You wanted a spot on the team and you got one," Cara said.

"Not by choice!" Jill protested. "You *know* it was an accident."

"I don't know anything. I only met you a few days ago," Cara said. "For all I know, you planned this from the very beginning."

Jill threw up her hands. "It was *your* idea to go sledding, not mine!"

"You were steering," Cara said bitterly. "Or pretending to, anyway."

Jill didn't know what else to say. "If it makes you feel better to go around hating my guts, go ahead. I have to shower and get to practice."

"Fine." Cara brushed a piece of lint off the bedspread. "Practice all you want."

"Fine. I will," Jill said, heading to the bathroom.

"But you won't be competing," Cara called.

Jill stopped and turned around. "Why not?"

"Because first thing this morning, I'm going to tell the USFSA the real truth about our accident," Cara said. "We'll see what they have to say. My bet is that you'll be off the team by this afternoon. And maybe you'll even be banned from competition for good!"

10
Tori

"**I**'m so glad Mom and Roger finally got out of our hair," Tori said. She followed Veronica and Natalia out of the hotel elevator early Tuesday morning. There was only one day to go until the short program.

Mrs. Carsen and Roger had gone for breakfast in town. Tori was relieved. Her mother had been driving her crazy. She never stopped giving orders or asking Tori how she felt.

Tori was even more relieved that she hadn't seen or heard from her father. Maybe he checked out, she thought. Maybe he was already halfway back to his home in Lake Placid.

The three girls walked into the hotel's casual dining room. It was open for breakfast and lunch only and catered to Western taste.

"I want a stack of pancakes," Natalia said. "With blueberries and maple syrup."

"I want a big bowl of cereal with a banana sliced onto it," Tori said.

"I want to get Evan back," Veronica said.

Tori shook her head. "Veronica, I already told you—"

"Oh, lighten up, Tori," Veronica interrupted her. "It is totally your fault that Evan broke up with me. But I forgive you."

"Thanks a lot," Tori said. "That's a big relief." She rolled her eyes.

"I think Evan would have found out my real age sooner or later, even if you hadn't blabbed," Veronica said. "I just wish I could have told him myself. I was going to, you know. I was tired of lying."

"Why don't you tell Evan that?" Tori asked.

"I tried!" Veronica said. "I called his dorm a million times. He wouldn't come to the phone."

"Why don't you write to him?" Tori said. "That way you can think really carefully about what you want to say. And even if he doesn't take you back, he'll hear your side of the story."

"Hmm. That's not a bad idea," Veronica murmured.

"Could we eat now?" Natalia cut in. "My stomach doesn't care about Evan. It only cares about pancakes."

The three girls smiled. They headed for an empty table by the window. Tori was walking past a small table when she noticed a familiar face.

"Jelena! Hi!" Tori stopped beside her table. "When's your practice?"

"At noon," Jelena said, putting down the book she was reading. "I thought I would have a good breakfast early. So . . . maybe you would like to sit here also?" She glanced up at Natalia. She looked almost shy.

"Sure," Natalia said. She looked surprised, Tori thought.

"You seem to be having a good time," Jelena said as they pulled their chairs up to the table.

"I always have a good time with Tori," Natalia said. She snapped open a napkin and put it in her lap. "And sometimes I even have a good time with Veronica."

"Thanks," Veronica said, scowling. Natalia grinned.

"So, Tori, you and Veronica are sisters, but you don't look alike," Jelena said.

"Veronica isn't really my sister," Tori said. She glanced at Veronica. "What are you? My stepsister?"

Veronica shrugged. "My mother divorced my father and married Roger. Then my mom divorced Roger, and he married Tori's mother."

"Oh. I see," Jelena said. She looked puzzled. "So you have many people living at your house?"

"It's a big house," Natalia said. "You got the pictures I sent, right?"

"Yes." Jelena nodded. "So what have you guys been doing? I have not seen you much, Natalia, since we got here."

"I know," Natalia said. "Too bad you aren't on the

same floor as us, Jelena. We had a riot last night. We all did French braids in each other's hair.''

"I think my hair is still tangled, Natalia." Tori ran her hands through her curly blond hair. "Thanks to you!"

Jelena stirred sugar into her tea and stared into the cup.

"We should have called you," Natalia said. She turned to Tori and Veronica. "Jelena does the best braids."

Jelena cleared her throat. "Not that I could have come. I was exercising."

"Wow. Exercising at night?" Tori asked. "How come?"

"I do some weight lifting—nothing too serious. And some ballet. It calms me down." Jelena took a sip of water.

"Jelena has a million little strategies for winning," Natalia said.

"So? There is no law against that," Jelena said.

"I didn't say there was anything wrong with it," Natalia said. "You're just superstitious, that's all."

"And you're not?" Jelena retorted.

"Whatever works best," Tori said in a bright voice, trying to steer the two sisters away from a fight. "We all have lucky routines that we do before a competition."

Neither Jelena nor Natalia said anything.

"So, uh, what's your favorite part of the Olympics so far?" Tori asked Jelena.

"Seeing my father is nice," Jelena said with a shrug. "Although he has been very busy going to meetings."

"You knew he'd be busy here," Natalia said.

"Yes. Of course I knew. He has been too busy all the time for me lately. But it can still bother me, can't it?" Jelena said tersely.

"What do you mean, he's been too busy?" Natalia asked.

"You two moved to America. After that I hardly ever see him," Jelena said.

"But that's not Papa's fault," Natalia argued. "He has to be in Washington for his job."

"*He* does, yes," Jelena agreed.

"What are you saying? Are you mad at me for leaving?" Natalia asked.

"Oh no," Tori moaned, cutting off Natalia. She hated to interrupt. But she had just spotted a familiar red ski sweater and a head of blond curly hair. It was him. Her so-called father. He *hadn't* left.

Tori sank down in her chair. "Why won't he go away?"

"What is it? Who are you hiding from?" Natalia asked, peering over her shoulder.

"It's the nightmare of the century," Tori mumbled. She stared at the table as her father walked over.

"Good morning, girls," he greeted them. "Sorry to barge in on your breakfast."

"That's okay," Veronica told him.

Tori looked at Veronica, raising one eyebrow. It wasn't okay. It was anything *but* okay!

"Tori, I'd like to talk to you. Do you have a minute?" Mr. Carsen asked.

"No," Tori said curtly. "I don't." Not for *you*, anyway! she almost added. She wasn't even going to look at him. He'd pretended she didn't exist for the past fifteen years. Now it was her turn to do the same.

"Won't you even look at me? Tori?" Mr. Carsen persisted.

"No. I'm trying to enjoy my breakfast. And then I have to go to practice, okay?" Tori stared straight ahead. Mr. Carsen stood at her side, shifting his weight on his feet.

"Please, Tori. There's something I need to say," her father pleaded.

"You said enough already," Tori snapped.

"Tori's just nervous. It's the last practice before the short program tomorrow night," Natalia explained. She nudged Tori's foot under the table. "I'm sure she didn't mean that."

Tori didn't say anything. Did Natalia expect her to apologize? To the man who left her when she was a baby? The same man who'd given her muscular dystrophy? Never. She didn't want to see him, hear from him, or talk to him, ever again.

"I thought you were leaving Japan," Tori said coldly. "Why are you still here?"

"Leave Japan? Now? But Tori, I couldn't leave," her father said, crouching beside her chair. "Not after our talk left you so upset. Couldn't we just talk for five minutes? I won't upset you again, I promise."

"Just listening to your voice upsets me, okay?" Tori said bitterly.

Veronica frowned. "Maybe later today would be a good time, Mr. Carsen," she suggested.

"What time today?" Mr. Carsen pressed.

"I don't know. How about never? Is that a good time for you?" Tori pushed her chair back from the table and stared at her father. "I told you once. Stay away from me!"

"I'm sorry," he said. "I didn't mean—"

"You didn't mean anything, according to you," Tori said. "You never mean anything. But you keep messing everything up for me anyway!" Tori tossed her napkin onto the table and raced for the elevator. She'd order room service from now on, if that was what it took to get him out of her life!

Natalia, Veronica, and Jelena dashed after her and jumped onto the elevator just before the doors closed. Tori punched the button for the twenty-second floor. Jelena reached over her shoulder and pushed the button for fifteen.

"You were so mean to him," Natalia said as the elevator began to rise. "I know he's not perfect, but he's your father."

"He isn't my father," Tori said. "I've only known Roger for about a year, and he's already more of a dad to me than that guy ever was."

"I don't think it's right to be so harsh to him," Natalia commented. "No matter what you say, he's your father. He loves you. Blood is . . . how do you say? Thicker than water."

"No. You don't understand." Tori shook her head. "Your father is wonderful. Mine isn't."

"Well, look at it this way," Natalia said. "It's lucky for me and Jelena that our father is a good parent, because he's the only parent we have."

The doors opened at the fifteenth floor. Jelena started to step out of the elevator, but stopped half-way.

"You mean it's lucky for *you*, Natalia. He's the only parent *you* have—and he's all yours," Jelena said angrily. "That's what I've been trying to tell you. Blood is not thicker than water. Papa is hardly a father to me! And lately, you are not a sister, either! Tori and Veronica aren't sisters at all, and they get along better than we do." She let go of the doors, and they slid closed. There was a long silence as the elevator rose.

"Wow," Tori finally said. "Did you know she felt that way?"

Natalia put her hands over her face. Veronica put an arm around her shoulders.

"I guess I had a feeling," Natalia said. She sighed. Tori saw that there were tears in her eyes. "But I didn't know she was so angry at me. Or so hurt about the fact that Papa and I moved to the U.S."

"Nat, you have to skip my practice and go talk to her," Tori said. "You have to fix this."

"I think I will wait a little while until she cools off,"

Natalia said as the elevator stopped on their floor. "Then I will talk to her."

"Good," Tori said. "Family is more important than anything, Nat. You guys have to work things out."

As the words left Tori's mouth, she realized she must sound two-faced. Here she was telling Natalia how important families were, but she couldn't stand the sight of her own father!

11

Tori

"**Y**ou looked much better today," Dan Trapp said as Tori stepped off the ice a few hours later.

"I felt much better," Tori said. She wiped the beads of sweat off her forehead with a towel. In fact, she had felt great out there. She'd landed every jump cleanly. She could have skated for at least another hour.

Tori didn't tell Dan why she had skated so well. Every time she pictured her father's face, she felt a surge of anger. And it seemed as if the anger made her stronger.

"I have to admit, I was concerned yesterday," Dan said. "You didn't have a very good practice. But you put all my fears to rest today." He squeezed Tori's shoulders. "The moment's almost here. I'm so proud of you."

"Thanks," Tori said. She leaned against Dan. She'd never had a coach she liked working with so much—or a coach who had more faith in her.

"You know what to do this afternoon," Dan said. "Rest. Stretch. Take a hot bath. And visualize your program. Your perfect, *winning* program."

Tori nodded. "Okay." She turned to head for the locker room and nearly crashed into Natalia. "Hey! You made it after all." Tori laughed, feeling exhilarated after her practice. "So," she added, remembering Natalia's problem, "did you talk to Jelena?"

"She wasn't there. You know how I was saying that she has a bunch of weird traditions? Well, she gets superstitious about seeing the ice she's going to compete on the day before the competition," Natalia explained.

"So how's she going to practice?" Tori asked, glancing at the clock on the wall. "I thought the Russian team was coming in at noon."

"Everyone else is, but not Jelena. To focus, she always goes somewhere else, where nobody knows her, and there are no judges or coaches around. She skates by herself," Natalia explained. "When I went to her room, she was already gone. Papa told me she went off to the public rink. I am going to find her there. I came by to see if you want to go."

"To the public rink in Nagano? Now?" Tori pulled a heavy sweatshirt over her skating dress. "I don't know. I should go back to our room and lie down for a while. I had a great practice, and I don't want to jinx it by skating any more today."

"Oh." Natalia's face fell. "Are you sure? Afterward we could all have hot chocolate or hot sushi or whatever they drink here. Wait—not sushi—sake! No, wait—sake is wine. We're definitely not having that. But could you come? You don't have to skate."

Tori hesitated. "Maybe . . . I don't know."

"Tori, I know you need to take it easy," Natalia said. "But it would be a big help to me if you came along. I am so awkward talking to Jelena lately." She scuffed the floorboard with her sneaker.

Tori could see that Natalia was still struggling to find a way to talk to her sister. "I can't promise anything right now," she said. "But if I feel better after I take a nap, I'll come meet you. Okay?"

"Thanks. That's good enough for me," Natalia said with a grin. "Papa said Jelena would be at the public rink for a couple of hours. Come down after you have rested—please?" She clasped her hands together.

"I'll try," Tori promised. "Now I'd better get back to the hotel before my mother launches a search party!"

Tori unwrapped the towel from her head and started to brush her long, blond hair. She must have soaked in the big hotel bathtub for an hour, lying still and doing Dan's visualization exercises. She felt calm and relaxed.

If only the short program were tonight, instead of tomorrow night, she thought. The way her health had been lately, she never knew how she would feel from one day to the next. She didn't want to take a chance by waiting.

She sat down on her bed and turned on the television, flipping to the Olympic Coverage Channel. The station broadcast Olympic news all day long, in English. While she got dressed, she listened to a story about snowboarding making its debut as an Olympic sport. The story ended. An anchor came on to give a recap of the day's top stories. Tori scooped up her tiny pearl earrings from the bedside table and put them on as she watched.

"And now, a very special, exclusive interview. One of the most touching stories to come from the Nagano Olympics is that of Tori Carsen. This promising young figure skater's seemingly endless future of medals has been cut short. She received a diagnosis of myotonic muscular dystrophy just a month before the Olympics."

Tori dropped an earring onto the carpet. Why were they doing a story all about her? And why did they have to focus on her illness?

"Our reporter spoke to Tori's father this morning," the anchor continued, as Tori leaned over to pick up her earring. "And here is that interview with James Carsen, in its entirety."

Tori sat bolt upright, knocking her head against the

bed frame. What? Her father was giving an exclusive interview about her? He barely knew her!

The TV image switched from the anchor's desk to the snow-covered ice arena, the White Ring. "A daughter is precious," a reporter's voice said, as sappy music played. "And even more precious is the daughter that the father never got a chance to know . . . until now," the reporter went on.

Tori stared at the television, stunned. The picture shifted to the reporter, standing next to her father outside the arena. Tori felt as if she were going to burst from anger. Since when did he have the right to talk about her as if he knew her?

"According to James Carsen, Tori's chances of winning an Olympic medal grow dimmer with each day that passes. Tori is suffering from the horrible disease of muscular dystrophy."

"Shut up!" Tori screamed at the screen. "It's not like that!" She did have a chance to medal—Dan said so, Natalia said so, everyone said so. How dare her father tell a reporter otherwise?

"What brought you to Nagano?" the reporter asked, holding the microphone to Mr. Carsen. "After all these years of separation, what made you decide to contact your daughter now?"

"I had to see Tori. I wanted to see her skate, but I also needed to talk to her about the muscular dystrophy. It's a genetically inherited disease. My mother passed it on to me, and I passed it on to Tori. I have such a mild case, I didn't think about it when my wife and I had Tori."

"That's the truth," Tori seethed, glaring at him. "Because you never think about anything but yourself!"

"How *is* Tori?" the reporter asked. "Should we be rooting for her to win the gold . . . or rooting for her health?"

"Her health seems pretty good. But she's weaker than I expected," Mr. Carsen said. "Sometimes this disease strikes fast. In Tori's case it seems to be doing that. I'm afraid her skating career may come to an end sooner than she thinks."

"You don't know anything!" Tori cried. She clicked the remote, shutting off the TV. Tori couldn't take any more. She had to get out of the hotel suite. She needed some fresh air.

Tori strode through the living room to her mother and Roger's bedroom. She was about to open the door and ask if anyone wanted to go for a walk when she heard them talking.

"I can't believe he'd do an interview like that," her mother was saying. "They must have paid him. I wouldn't put it past him to take money for talking about his child."

"I can't believe he thinks that *this* is the way to get involved in Tori's life," Roger said.

"That's just it—that's what I've been trying to tell Tori. He *doesn't* think!" Mrs. Carsen said. "Now he's totally disrupting her life. She's too fragile, Roger. She can't handle all the stress of the Olympics as it is!"

Tori turned away from the door. She couldn't handle all the stress? Was that what her mother thought? She'd been handling more stress than anyone could possibly imagine. And now not even her mother believed in her!

It was true that sometimes Tori felt fragile and weak. But she could still skate. She'd had a fantastic practice today. Now everyone thought she was going to collapse on the ice.

I'm not going to crumple, Tori told herself. I won't let them all be right.

She grabbed her skate bag and a jacket and walked out the door, closing it quietly behind her. All she needed was a little extra practice time with Jelena. She'd show everyone how fragile she was—by winning a medal!

12
Tori

"**H**ello," Tori said. "This goes downtown, right?"

She started climbing up the steps of the city bus. The next hotel shuttle into town wasn't for another half an hour. Tori hadn't felt like waiting. She had walked a few blocks to reach a public bus stop.

She hoped Jelena was still skating at the public rink. She also hoped that Natalia had already talked to her. She didn't want to show up in the middle of anything, but she just *had* to get out of her hotel room. She was so angry at her father she couldn't sit still.

The Japanese driver shook his head and pointed to the rear of the bus.

"I don't understand," Tori said. "It doesn't go downtown? But the sign said . . ."

The driver pointed to the back doors again and frowned.

"But I need to get on. I have the fare right here!" Tori waved her money in the air.

The bus driver started closing the doors—right in Tori's face.

"You must get on the bus at the back," said a Japanese woman who had just stepped off the bus.

"Oh! It's backwards," Tori said. Then she realized how that sounded. "Not backwards as in backwards—just . . . opposite! Not the same."

The woman stared at her. "The bus will leave soon. You must hurry."

Tori rushed to the rear doors of the bus and climbed on, depositing her fare. Then she looked around for a seat. As soon as she sat down, she pulled out the map she had gotten with her Olympic packet. Maybe she should have asked for directions at the hotel, but how hard could it be to find something as big as an ice rink? She studied the map for a second. There was the rink. It looked as if she were headed in the right direction.

Tori sat back in her seat and relaxed. She felt some of the tension drain out of her shoulders. It was fun, being out by herself, exploring. She hardly ever got to see more than the ice arenas in the cities where she competed. She was going to enjoy every second of Nagano's beautiful scenery.

"Okay, lady. End, end!" the bus driver said in English over the loudspeaker. "You get off now."

Tori blinked and rubbed her eyes. She had fallen asleep! She looked around the bus. She was the only passenger left. She stared out the bus window at a row of big warehouses and giant, empty parking lots.

"I was looking for the skating rink," Tori told the bus driver. She picked up her skate bag and walked to the front of the bus.

"Good-bye, lady!" he said cheerily.

"But I . . . I can't get off. I need to go back *there*." Tori pointed out the back of the bus. "To the ice rink!"

"On in back, off in front. Yes." He nodded. "Good-bye!"

Tori headed down the steps of the bus. She was trying not to get scared. She wasn't in any danger, she told herself. She simply needed to catch the next bus going in the opposite direction.

She crossed the deserted street, looking around nervously. She looked for a bus-stop sign. She didn't find one on the first block, so she kept walking until she saw a bus bench. She sat down and pulled her parka tightly around her in the cold winter air.

About twenty minutes later, a bus pulled up. Tori got on and collapsed into a seat in the back. After heading straight for a while, the bus veered to the right. It was going directly away from the city! Oh, no, Tori thought. What have I gotten myself into?

Tori gathered her courage.

"Um, does anyone here speak English?" she asked, looking around at the other passengers.

"I do," a woman said in a German accent.

"What do you need?" a Scottish man asked.

"I'm trying to go to the skating rink," Tori said. "Not the Olympic arena—the public rink in Nagano."

"You're a skater, then?" the Scottish man asked.

"Yes. I'm on the United States team," Tori said.

"Ah, but isn't skating a bonny sport. All you little girls out there, twirling about, light as a feather."

Tori smiled politely at him. That wasn't the way it was at all, but she didn't have time to explain. "So do you know where the rink is?"

"Let me check my guidebook." The German woman flipped through the pages. "Do you know the name of the rink? According to this, there are three public rinks in town."

"*Three?* Can I see?" Tori took the book and stared at it. There *were* three listings. One of the rinks was advertised as being close to the Olympic Village. She decided that had to be the one. "Okay, I think it's this one. But how do I get there?" she asked, holding up the guidebook.

"Ask the bus driver," the Scottish man said. "He's quite knowledgeable. Told me the latest yen exchange rate when I asked."

"You speak Japanese?" Tori asked eagerly. "Could you ask him the directions and write them down in English for me? Please?"

"Certainly," he said. "Hang on just a moment and we'll have you headed the right way. Wouldn't want an Olympic skater to be left out in the cold!"

Two hours later, Tori wandered around the skating rink, looking for her friends. It was growing dark. Tori had checked everywhere, but there was no sign of Natalia or Jelena.

She glanced at her watch. She'd spent ages getting to the rink—maybe she was too late. They had probably left. It didn't matter. Tori felt so exhausted, she didn't have the energy to skate. She just wanted to go back to the hotel and get into bed.

Tori reached into her pocket for some money, so she could catch the bus back to the hotel. She pulled out her wallet and thumbed through it. It was empty. She must have spent her last yen to get into the rink!

She hurried over to the entrance. "I can't stay," she said. "My friends aren't here, so I'm leaving. Is there any way you could give me my money back?"

A petite Japanese woman stared back at her. "No English," she said.

"Money. Yen," Tori said. She held up her wallet. "I gave you some just ten minutes ago, and now I need it back."

"No speak English," the woman said.

"Never mind." Tori sighed. Now she was really in trouble, she thought as she walked away. She had no way of getting home and no money. And nobody understood her language.

She had one option left. She had to call her mother. She hated having to ask to be rescued. She'd get lectured about running around the day before the short program. Her mother was probably worried because she hadn't left a note saying where she was.

Tori took a deep breath and picked up the pay phone. It was the only thing she could do.

She studied the directions on the telephone. Everything was written in Japanese! She scanned the list of options, but they were all foreign. Tori slammed the receiver back onto the phone and headed for the exit. She had no idea what she was going to do next. But standing in the ice rink wasn't helping her.

She walked outside and stared at the mountains on the horizon. From the hotel, the mountains were directly north. If she headed that way, it shouldn't take too long to get there. But the way her muscles felt, she wasn't sure how far she could walk.

If only her father hadn't done that dumb interview, she wouldn't have gotten so angry that she had to leave the hotel. It was his fault she was out here in the first place. Everything was his fault—everything!

As Tori walked, her body ached more and more with each step. The muscles in her legs felt cramped and cold. Her skate bag felt as though it were filled with bricks. She kept moving it from one hand to the other, but she could barely carry it.

Spotting a bench up ahead, Tori decided to stop and rest for a minute. She sank onto the bench, her legs wobbly. Tori pulled her jacket sleeves over her hands and stuck them under her arms, shivering. She bounced her legs up and down, trying to warm up.

She couldn't believe it. She was at the Olympics. It was supposed to be the high point of her life. But here she was, sitting on a bench, alone, who knew where, cold, tired, and miserable!

She closed her mouth to keep her teeth from chattering and put her skate bag on her lap. "This is the stupidest thing I've ever done," she muttered.

"Tori? Are you all right?" a voice said.

Tori stared up at the figure looming over the end of the bench.

"Oh, no!" she cried. "What are *you* doing here?"

13
Tori

"I should ask you the same thing," Mr. Carsen said. "Tori, you're freezing! Here, take my coat." He slipped the heavy wool overcoat over her shoulders.

Tori didn't know whether to run away from her father or hug him. She would have been thankful to see anyone she knew. Anyone but him.

"You look exhausted," Mr. Carsen said. "Did you get lost?"

Tori nodded. "I was trying to find the public skating rink. I was supposed to meet my friends there. But I got on the wrong bus, and . . . anyway, never mind. I have to go."

Tori stood up and started walking down the sidewalk. She didn't know where she was going, but she had to get away from her father. She hated him!

"Tori, I know you're angry at me because of our

conversation," Mr. Carsen said, hurrying after her. "But please, let me take you back to the hotel. . . ." He took her arm.

Tori shook his hand off and kept walking. "I'll go by myself," Tori told him. "Stay away from me!" She walked faster even though her muscles ached. She had no idea where she was going. She just knew she couldn't stay on the same sidewalk with James Carsen for another minute!

"Tori, you're going in the wrong direction. The hotel's this way," Mr. Carsen said. "Please, let me walk you back. You shouldn't be out here, when it's so cold and damp. I'm worried about you."

Tori whirled around. "Since when do you worry about me? You've *never* cared about me!" She tossed off his coat, and it fell onto the sidewalk.

"Wh-What?" her father stammered. "Tori, of course I care." He leaned down to pick up his overcoat. "I care about you more than you'll ever know."

"Really? Then why did you give that dumb TV interview? Why did you say all that stuff about how weak I am?" Tori felt hot tears prickle her eyelids. "That wasn't fair. It isn't even *true*. I'm not weak. But how would you know that? You've never been part of my life. Never!"

"I'm sorry, Tori. But I—I just wanted a chance to tell my side of the story," Mr. Carsen said.

"Your side? Since when do you get a *side*?" Tori demanded.

Her father's eyes widened in surprise. He looked hurt.

"You show up here, out of the blue, and expect to be involved in my life!" Tori shouted. "It doesn't work like that!"

Mr. Carsen hung his head, nodding. "You're right. But when I heard about your illness, I felt responsible. I felt as if coming here might make it up to you somehow. I could explain."

"Explain what?" Tori stared angrily at him. "Explain why I'm sick? There *is* no explanation."

"I thought maybe I could help," her father added.

"The doctors don't have a cure, and neither do you," Tori shouted. "I'm stuck with this problem that you gave me. I have to deal with it now. And I don't need you going around telling reporters how weak I am!" Tears filled her eyes.

"I didn't mean it to sound so bad. I'm sorry about the interview—it was a stupid idea," Mr. Carsen said. "Tori, I know it sounds crazy, but I felt desperate to talk about you with somebody. Even if it sounded like I doubted your ability, I don't, Tori. Not anymore. I saw your practice this morning."

"No, you didn't. You weren't there!" Tori said.

"I *was* there," Mr. Carsen said. "I know you told me to stay away. But I wanted so badly to see you skate. I stood behind a pillar. I saw you skate, and it . . . it amazed me. You're so good. I was so proud."

Tori felt a surge of pleasure at her father's compliments. But she didn't want to forgive him just because he was finally trying to be nice.

"Then why did you tell that reporter I was weak?" Tori asked.

"That was before I saw you skate. I underestimated you," Mr. Carsen said, shrugging. "I won't let it happen again, believe me."

Tori kicked at a pebble on the sidewalk. Her leg felt heavy and tired. Tori's father was finally making the effort to really know her. She wasn't sure how she felt about it. Wasn't it too late? She was still angry with him. But maybe he deserved a second chance. Or was this the third chance? she wondered. How many chances do you give a person?

"Tori, I realize I don't really know you. I accept the blame for that," her father said, stepping closer. "But I'd like to get to know you better, starting now."

Tori thought it over for a minute. Whenever her mother talked about her father, she made him sound like the most irresponsible person on earth. He wasn't a saint, that was for sure. But maybe he wasn't *that* bad.

"I'm glad you're here—or at least, I was at first," Tori said slowly. "I was really excited when I first saw you. But then you and Mom fought. And you dropped that bombshell on me about how bad my muscular dystrophy will get. Couldn't that have waited until I got home? Until *after* I skated?" Tori asked. She looked up at him and brushed the tears from her eyes.

"Probably. No, you're right. I definitely should have waited. I just felt so guilty. I guess I thought it would help if you knew more about my mother. She was a wonderful person, Tori. And the muscular dystrophy never changed that. I tried to tell you that. But instead of helping you, I ruined everything." Tori's father shook his head. "I'm . . . I'm *so* sorry, Tori. I made a mistake. A big one."

Tori didn't know what to say. At least her father was finally being honest and owning up to his mistakes.

"Anyway, we'd better get you back to the hotel right away," Mr. Carsen said. "Your mother is worried sick. When she told me you were missing, I went out and started looking for you. Would you share a cab with me, or do you want your own?" he asked Tori.

"I'll share a taxi with you," Tori said. She couldn't wait to sit down and rest her aching body. She felt as if she couldn't walk another step. "I don't hate you that much."

"But close?" Her father smiled as he hailed a taxi.

Tori wasn't sure how she felt. But she was willing to forgive her father—as long as he didn't hurt her again. "Let's just take it one step at a time, okay? Starting with the short program tomorrow night. I do want you there," she told him. "But to be on the safe side, you'd better not sit with my mom. I might have forgiven you, but she won't."

He nodded. "I know. Thanks, Tori."

"You're welcome," Tori said. "Just don't do any more interviews about me, okay?"

Mr. Carsen raised his eyebrows. "Not even when you win a medal?"

"Not even then," Tori said. "Unless you say something like, 'I always knew she could do it.' "

"Maybe not always, but I know that now," Mr. Carsen said. He held open the taxi door and Tori climbed in. He stepped in after her and told the driver something in Japanese. They had a brief conversation, and then the car pulled away from the curb.

Tori stared at her father. "You speak Japanese?"

Mr. Carsen shrugged. "A little. Hey, there are lots of things you don't know about *me*," he said.

"Wow! I guess not," Tori said.

"I'm fine, Mom. Nothing happened," Tori said with a sigh. She'd been explaining her afternoon to Roger and her mother for the past half hour. Well, not everything—she decided not to tell her mother that she'd worked things out with her dad. It would only make Mrs. Carsen more upset than she already was.

"I just made some mistakes, that's all," Tori told her and Roger. "I ran out without thinking because I got cabin fever. It's no big deal."

"So you'll go to your room and take a hot bath and have a nap. Right away. You promise?" Mrs. Carsen said.

Tori rolled her eyes. Why did her mother insist on treating her like a two-year-old whenever she was worried? "Yes, Mom, I promise. And then I'll have a graham cracker and drink tea with my teddy bear."

Roger laughed. "Can I have a graham cracker too?"

"Call me when the hot cocoa is ready. I'll break out the Chutes and Ladders," Veronica said from her spot on the couch.

Tori giggled and Mrs. Carsen reached out and stroked her cheek. "I'm sorry. I was just worried. I don't mean to treat you like a baby."

"It's okay, Mom." Tori stood up and kissed her mother on the cheek. "Come over later, okay?" She headed through the living room toward her bedroom and opened the door. She couldn't wait to slip into her flannel pajamas and—

"You're the one who's selfish," Jelena was yelling at Natalia. "All you can think about is you and Tori and—" Jelena stopped talking when she saw Tori.

"Oh, excuse me," Tori mumbled.

"It's okay," Natalia said, standing up. "You can come in."

"We should discuss this in private," Jelena argued.

"We can speak in front of Tori. She's like family," Natalia said.

"She's not family to me," Jelena muttered.

"Look, I can go away—" Tori began.

"No," Natalia said firmly. She faced Jelena and crossed her arms in front of her. "Don't go anywhere. This is your room, too."

Tori glanced at Jelena. She was staring back at Natalia. "So," Tori said, trying to relax the atmosphere.

"Did you guys find the rink? Did you get a chance to skate?"

"Yes. Natalia came with her skates," Jelena said. "She wanted to show me how good she is."

"What? That's not why I came," Natalia said.

"It isn't?" Jelena replied.

"No! I came to *talk* to you. Only you wouldn't listen to me," Natalia said.

Jelena stood up and walked over to the window. "Why should I?"

"Because we're sisters," Natalia said. "Because I can't stand us fighting. Please, Jelena. Tell me what's wrong!"

Jelena was silent for a moment. When she turned to face Tori and Natalia, her face was streaked with tears. "When you and Papa left to live in America, I didn't want to go. But now I see I should have."

"Why?" Natalia asked. "I thought you liked training in Moscow."

"I do. But I lost my whole family. First Mama died. And now you and Papa are gone." Jelena's voice shook. "But even though we are far apart on the map, I thought we were still close. Here. Where it counts." She tapped her chest. "Now I see I was wrong. Because you do not even think of me as your sister anymore. You have a new sister—Tori!" Jelena buried her face in her hands and sobbed.

Tori gasped. "Me? But Jelena, I'm not—I could never—you don't understand. All Natalia ever talks about is *you* and your grandmother and how much she misses both of you."

Natalia walked over to Jelena and took her hand. "Tori is not my sister," she said softly. *"You* are."

"But you do not act that way. Ever since you got here! You watch *her* practice, you stay in *her* room, you eat breakfast with her—you live with her now. You don't need me. You don't want me around," Jelena said. She wiped the tears off her face with the sleeve of her sweater.

"Jelena. Maybe I have acted . . . distant," Natalia admitted. "But that was only because *you* acted that way—from the moment we saw each other at the train station! I could tell you didn't even want to hug me!"

"What am I supposed to do? You show up with Tori. You are best friends. You know everything about each other. I feel like . . . like a stranger," Jelena said.

"Well, it's true, Tori and I are close. But it's your fault, too. You never wrote back to me. That's why I stopped writing," Natalia said.

"I never wrote back because all your letters were always about Tori, and your other new friends. I felt so left out," Jelena said.

"I wasn't trying to leave you out. I was trying to include you in my new life!" Natalia explained. "I'm so sorry." Her voice caught, and she reached out and hugged her older sister.

"It's okay," Jelena said, squeezing her tightly. "I am sorry too."

Tori turned and started to tiptoe out of the room. She could tell the sisters still had a lot of talking to do.

"Wait, Tori," Jelena called.

Tori turned around. "I didn't mean to come between you guys or anything. I was just trying to be a good friend," she said.

"And you are a good friend. I can see that," Jelena said.

"Jelena, no matter how close Tori and I are as friends, you'll always be my big sister," Natalia said. "I think about you all the time. I wish we could live in the same place again. But for now, we have to learn how to get along in different worlds."

"You're right. But now we've wasted so much time arguing. We haven't been able to catch up at all!" Jelena complained.

"You still have time," Tori said. "We'll all be here four more days, right?"

"True. Hey, you want to sleep in Papa's and my suite tonight?" Jelena offered. "We might be talking all night. We don't want to bother you, Tori."

"That's really nice of you. But you know, you can't stay up all night, either," Tori reminded Jelena. "Not with our short programs tomorrow."

"This is the moment I have been dreading," Natalia confessed.

"Our short programs?" Jelena frowned at her. "You are dreading this?"

"Gee, thanks for the vote of confidence," Tori said.

"No, not your programs," Natalia said. "Just . . . I

love both of you. How can I root for one of you over the other?

"I know—how about a tie for the gold medal? Russia and America must split the medal in half."

Tori raised her eyebrows. "I'm superglad you guys made up, but don't be silly. I'm not splitting with anyone." She smiled and tried to look confident. But inside, she didn't feel that way. She couldn't remember her muscles ever hurting so badly. And she felt so tired that her vision was blurry.

"I am not splitting either!" Jelena replied. She and Tori smiled at each other.

"I have a very important appointment—with my pillow," Tori said. "So I'll let you two hang out."

"Thanks," Jelena said. "Good luck tomorrow."

"Same to you," Tori said. She yawned. She was so tired she could hardly keep her eyes open. Maybe she should take a hot bath first, to loosen up her muscles, she told herself. She could make the water really hot and soak forever. But the way she felt right now, forever still wouldn't be long enough. Tori knew that if she felt this way tomorrow, she wouldn't be able to skate her short program.

14
Jill

"**A**mber, is that you?" Jill asked. She and Tori were on two phones in Tori's hotel suite. They had arranged to call their friends back home in Pennsylvania. It was Wednesday afternoon. Tori was on the telephone in her bedroom, and Jill was on the extension in the living room.

"Hey, Jill! Hi, Tori!" Amber Armstrong said cheerfully. "We can't wait to see your short programs!"

Jill smiled. Amber didn't sound too upset about being at home when she could have been at the Olympics—if she weren't too young.

"Thanks," Tori said. "Any special plans?"

"Oh, yeah!" Amber cried. "We're having a big party and everyone in Silver Blades is meeting at Kathy's house to watch." Kathy Bart was one of the Silver Blades coaches.

"That sounds like fun," Jill said. "But don't let Kathy tell you guys what to do all night, okay?" Kathy was a tough coach. Lots of kids in Silver Blades called her Sarge behind her back.

Amber giggled. "Kathy already promised she wouldn't act like a coach. She said that she was off duty for the night."

"I bet she'll still critique our performances," Tori said.

"Probably," Amber said. "But we're all so excited that I don't think anyone's going to notice if you make a mistake—which you *won't*."

"Of course not!" Jill said. "We'll do our best!"

"I know. And Jill, I'm glad you got a chance to skate on the team," Amber said. "Too bad Cara got hurt. Are you really as evil as all the newspapers say?"

"No. I'm *worse*," Jill teased. She was trying to make light of the situation. She didn't want her friends to know how worried she was. But every time she thought of Cara filing a formal complaint against her, she felt sick to her stomach.

What if everyone believed Cara's story? The audience would boo her when she skated onto the ice. The judges would give her low marks. And if the USFSA decided she'd broken a rule, she might even be banned from competing in the future!

"Well, I hope you both do great," Amber said. "We're behind you a hundred million percent. Here's Nikki!"

"Hi, you guys!" Nikki Simon said brightly. Nikki

skated pairs in Silver Blades. She, Tori, and Jill had been friends for a long time.

"Hey, Nik, what time is it in Seneca Hills?" Jill asked.

"It's Tuesday night," Nikki said. "You wouldn't even be skating until tomorrow if you were here." Japan's time zone was eighteen hours ahead of the time zone in Pennsylvania. It was two o'clock in the afternoon in Japan, but only eight o'clock the night before in Pennsylvania.

"That would be nice—I could get in some more practice," Jill joked.

"And I could worry for another twenty-four hours. No thanks!" Tori said.

"Don't worry, Tori. If anyone can handle all the pressure, it's you," Nikki told her. "So are you guys having any fun?"

Jill sighed. "Yes and no. How about if we tell you the whole story when we get home?"

"Yeah," Tori agreed. "We have a lot to fill you in on."

"Okay. But take lots of pictures, okay? The ones they've had in the *Seneca Hills Sentinel* have all been blurry and horrible," Nikki said.

"That's because they can't get close enough to us to get a good picture. What with the huge crowds and all," Jill said.

"Oh, well, la-dee-da," Nikki said, laughing. "Hold on, here's Haley. Good luck, you guys. We love you!"

"Thanks!" Jill and Tori yelled into the phone. "I

wish they could be here," Tori said sadly. "It's not the same."

"I know," Jill agreed.

"Good afternoon, Japan!" Haley Arthur cried, coming onto the line. Haley also skated pairs in Silver Blades. She was the most wild and crazy friend Jill and Tori had. "You guys are not going to believe this. Everyone here is totally in love with all of you!"

"Everyone's in love with us?" Jill raised an eyebrow.

"You're on TV all the time," Haley continued. "They show you walking into practice, walking out of practice, brushing your teeth, flossing between your teeth. . . ."

"No way." Tori giggled.

"Not really," Haley said. "But close. Anyway, both of you knock 'em dead, okay? We're not meeting you at the airport unless we hear 'The Star-Spangled Banner' on the medal stand. And we don't mean for Tracy Wilkins!"

Jill unlocked the door to her room. She'd been wandering around the Olympic Village all afternoon. She was trying to get her mind off the short program that night and all the controversy about her and Cara. But now it was time to get her skate bag and her costume and head to the White Ring. Her mother was coming by in a minute. They'd go to the arena together.

She dropped her coat on the bed. She went into the bathroom to brush her hair. A pink piece of paper was stuck to the mirror. It was a note from Cara. Jill peeled it off and read it.

"Dear Jill," the note began. "Don't bother showing up tonight. My ankle is better, and I'll be skating after all. You can go back to being an alternate."

Jill crumpled the note in her hand. She couldn't believe it! How could Cara skate on that ankle?

There was a knock at the door, and Jill rushed to open it. Her mother stood in the hallway, with a smile on her face. Mrs. Wong had arrived a day earlier. Jill remembered the relief she'd felt when she saw her mother's face. She had never been so glad to see anyone.

"Ready to go?" Mrs. Wong asked.

"Read this!" Jill showed the crumpled note to her mother.

Mrs. Wong read the note. When she looked up at Jill, her eyes were flashing with anger. "What does she think she's doing?"

"I don't know, Mom, but I'm scared." Jill grabbed her skating dress from the closet and picked up her skate bag. "Cara told the USFSA that I hurt her ankle on purpose, to get onto the team. If they believe her, even a little bit . . ."

"Jill, be reasonable. They won't just take her word for it," Mrs. Wong said. "They'll find out what really happened. You will skate tonight."

"What if I can't?" Jill said. "What if they believe her?"

"They won't, honey," Mrs. Wong said.

"But Mom—" Jill started.

"Shhh." Jill's mother put a finger to Jill's lips. "No one is going to think you hurt Cara's ankle on purpose."

"I hope you're right, Mom," Jill said. "But we have to get to the rink and find Kate Vandervleet from the USFSA—now! Before Cara ruins my reputation even more than she already has!"

15
Tori

Tori walked into the locker room and sank down on a bench. She smoothed the skirt of her sea-foam green skating dress. She and several other skaters had just warmed up for the short program in front of thousands of fans. Tori was so nervous, she felt sick to her stomach. Tracy Wilkins was still out on the ice. Maybe I should be too, thought Tori.

She took a few deep breaths, trying to relax. The fact that she hadn't seen Jill yet was starting to worry her. Jill's warm-up period was next. If she didn't get here soon, she'd miss it.

Tori heard somebody walking into the locker room and looked up, hoping to see Jill.

"That arena is packed, isn't it?" Cara asked. She was wearing a purple skating dress with sequincovered sleeves. She was limping as she made her way to the mirror.

"Where's Jill?" Tori asked, standing up in shock. "Why are you dressed to compete?"

"My ankle's feeling much better. So Jill's not coming—I'm skating," Cara said.

"You are?" Tori was stunned. "But Jill said you couldn't even fit your ankle into your skate."

"Oh, Jill said that?" Cara snorted. "Figures. My ankle is a little sore. But I've skated with worse injuries." She fastened a delicate gold necklace with a heart-shaped locket around her neck. "Anyway, I've got my lucky necklace."

"A lucky necklace isn't going to help you." Jill marched into the room, her scarlet skating dress slung over one arm. Red was Jill's favorite color—most of her skating dresses were one shade of red or another. "What are you doing here?" she asked Cara, her hands on her hips.

"What I came here to do." Cara pulled up her tights, smoothing them on her legs. "Skate."

"Cara, come on. You're in no condition to skate," Jill said. "You'll jeopardize your own health—your own future—if you go out there."

"You mean I'll jeopardize *your* future, don't you?" Cara asked.

"Cara! Be reasonable," Tori said. "If you compete, you'll ruin the team's chances at a medal."

Cara scowled at Tori. "Who cares about the stupid

team? I'm the one who deserves an Olympic medal. I'm the one who's waited for this the longest! And I won't get another chance. This is supposed to be my year.''

Tori didn't know what to say. She couldn't help feeling bad for Cara. She knew what it was like to think of never getting another chance to compete at the Olympics. She was in the same position.

But it was clear that Cara couldn't medal, even if she did skate. Tori doubted she'd be able to land even one jump.

"Hello, girls. Mind if I come in?"

Tori turned around and saw Kate Vandervleet standing in the doorway. Tori looked at Jill and bit her lip.

"Nice to see you all," Mrs. Vandervleet said. "Cara, we've reviewed your complaint against Jill."

Tori stared at the official. If Mrs. Vandervleet was here to tell Jill that she couldn't skate, Tori was going to be furious. Jill was healthy—Jill deserved to skate. Not Cara.

"Cara, I see you've got your skates on. You're dressed to compete," Mrs. Vandervleet said. "Jill told us you left her a note saying you planned to skate. I was very surprised."

"My ankle's much better. It's fine, in fact." Cara smiled. "I'm ready to skate!"

"I'm so glad it feels better," Mrs. Vandervleet said. "But Cara, we've spoken to the doctor who examined you. Your ankle is badly sprained. The doctor says there's no way you can skate. And your coach agrees."

"It *was* bad. But I've been icing it and staying off it. I know I can go out there," Cara said.

"We've already made our decision, and we're sticking by it," Mrs. Vandervleet said. She crossed her arms over her plaid jacket. "Jill will be skating tonight, in your place. I'm sorry, but that's the way it has to be. I know this is a huge disappointment to you." She reached out for Cara, to give her a comforting hug. Cara pushed her away.

Jill quickly started changing from her clothes into her scarlet skating dress. Tori pulled Jill's skates from her bag and handed them to Jill.

"Hurry, Jill!" Tori said. "Your warm-up is going to start any second!"

Jill finished dressing and sat down to lace up her skates.

Cara watched Jill for a minute, then turned back to Mrs. Vandervleet. "What about how she injured me?" She pointed at Jill. "How can you let her skate? She shouldn't even be an alternate, never mind *on* the U.S. team."

"Cara, we spoke to some people who were on the slope when your sled crashed. We've heard both sides of the story," Mrs. Vandervleet explained patiently.

"Both sides? What about my side? You've barely listened to that!" Cara protested.

"Based on what the witnesses said, we believe that the sled accident was exactly that—an *accident*. It wasn't Jill's fault. When a competitor is injured and unable to compete, the alternate fills in. That's the way it's done."

Cara whirled around and pointed to Tori. "What about *her*? She's sick. Kick her off the team—not me!"

Tori gasped. "Me?" She never imagined that Cara would turn on her.

"Cara!" Mrs. Vandervleet said sternly. "That is completely out of order! Tori isn't part of this. And besides, she's in excellent shape!"

"So am I!" Cara cried. "And I want to compete. It's not *fair*!"

"Injuries are never fair. Accepting them is part of being a good sport," Mrs. Vandervleet said.

"Tell *Jill* about being a good sport. Tell her that deliberately knocking someone out of the competition is *not* being a good sport!" Cara shouted. She stormed out of the dressing room, limping on her hurt ankle.

"You believe it was an accident, don't you, Mrs. Vandervleet?" Jill asked. She looked up nervously as she put on a pair of tiny ruby earrings.

"Yes, I do, Jill. Now, try to get all of this out of your mind. You have a program to skate. Good luck, Jill and Tori—we're all pulling for you." Mrs. Vandervleet turned around and walked out.

"I don't know if she's glad I'm skating or not," Jill said. "She's probably upset because Cara's off the team. And Cara's the one the Olympic Committee went out of their way to get," Jill added. "Everyone wants to see her skate instead of me—I know that."

"Jill! Come on, snap out of it," Tori said. "Cara complained about you, but it didn't work. *You're* skating. Now hurry up or you'll miss your warm-up!" She tugged on Jill's sleeve.

A few minutes later, they walked to the rink's edge. All of the skaters in Jill's warm-up group were already on the ice. Jill handed her skate guards to Tori and stepped onto the ice.

Dozens of other skaters were pacing around, waiting for the event to begin. Tracy Wilkins was drinking spring water from a bottle, and her hand was shaking from nerves.

Tori watched Jill speed across the ice. She saw Jill's coach, Ludmila, standing farther down the boards, calling out directions to Jill.

A few minutes later, the announcer spoke over the P.A. system. She spoke Japanese first, then switched to English.

"Skaters on the ice, your warm-up period is over. Please clear the ice," she said. "Good evening, ladies and gentlemen. Welcome to the women's figure-skating competition."

The crowd roared, applauding and whistling. Spectators waved flags from different nations back and forth, shouting support for their teams.

"Tonight, the women will skate the short program, which counts for one-third of the final score."

The butterflies in Tori's stomach started to multiply. She chewed a fingernail, looking around for Dan. If she'd ever needed a visualization technique to calm her down, it was now.

Jill skated over and walked through the opening in the boards. Tori handed Jill her skate guards.

"Sorry to be such a flake," Jill said, as she slipped them on. "I was just so crushed when I got the note Cara left me. I thought it was all over. I had to find Mrs. Vandervleet and tell her about the note. But when she walked into the locker room, I was afraid she was going to be glad that Cara was skating. And I thought she would say that the USFSA wanted to suspend *me* because of the sled accident."

"Well, she didn't," Tori told her. She paced back and forth by the boards.

Jill leaned against the boards and yawned.

"Jill! How can you be so calm? You're skating first!" Tori said.

"I guess I feel as if I have nothing to lose. I didn't even know I'd be skating until two days ago. I haven't had as much pressure on me as you have." Jill shook out her arms, then crouched down, stretching the back of her calf and thigh muscles.

"True," Tori said. "But you're still a rock, Jill. I wish I could be like you."

"No, you don't. I don't have as good a chance of winning as you do," Jill told her.

"Thanks. I needed that." Tori managed a small smile. "Where's your mother?"

Jill gazed at the packed stands. "I don't know. I wish I knew where she's sitting. After all the accusations Cara made, I feel like everyone here is rooting against me, except you and Mom and Ludmila."

"Don't think that way. You might have to win a couple of them over, but you can do that when you skate," Tori said.

"Jill." Ludmila walked over to her. "That was a nice warm-up. How do you feel?"

"Scared!" Jill said. "But if I can just sit down and breathe for a few minutes I'll be fine—"

Static over the public address system cut Jill off.

"Our first competitor in the women's short program is Cara Hopkins—excuse me." The announcer cleared her throat. "Not Cara Hopkins. Jill Wong! Skating for the United States."

"Forget about sitting down. Good luck, Jill!" Tori gave her a quick hug. Then she picked up her jacket, grabbed her Walkman from her skate bag, and rushed away from the ice. She hoped Jill did well, but she couldn't bear to watch!

16
Tori

Tori closed the stall door behind her and sat down on the closed toilet lid. She didn't know whether she wanted to cry or throw up. She was nervous and upset. She didn't know how she was going to make it through her short program.

You've skated that program a hundred times, Tori told herself. A thousand times.

Focus on something else, she thought, slipping the headphones over her ears. She started playing the tape Dan had made for her, filled with relaxing sounds of crashing waves and chirping birds. She remembered how skeptical she'd been when he gave it to her.

"How is pretending I'm at the beach going to help me skate? Are you crazy?" she'd said. But it worked— usually.

Tori had been sitting in the bathroom for about five

minutes when she heard someone knocking on the stall door. She slipped off the headphones. "Hello?" she said timidly.

"Tori? Are you in there?" It was Jill, gasping and out of breath.

"How did you know I was here?" Tori unlocked the door and walked out.

"Because, you always take off before you have to skate," Jill said. "Are you okay?"

"I'm fine. Forget about me. How about *you*? How did it go?" Tori grasped her friend's arm.

"Well . . ." Jill paused for a moment. Then her face broke into a wide grin. "I did okay. Not quite great, but really good. Mostly five-sevens."

"That's awesome!" Tori told her. "Especially considering you were the first skater out there. You know the judges give low marks at the beginning, so they can leave room for the rest of us."

Jill nodded. "I know. I think I'll turn out okay. Maybe not the very top, but I could still have a shot at a medal."

Tori felt awkward about the fact that when she stepped on the ice, she'd be trying to do better than Jill. It would have been much easier if Cara were the one she had to beat, instead of one of her best friends. But competing against friends was something all of Tori's friends had gotten used to.

"I'm glad you did well, Jill," she told her friend. "It makes it a little easier for me to go out there."

"I would have done better, only I couldn't stop

thinking about Cara, and how upset she was," Jill said.

"It's not your fault, Jill. She can skate in another Olympics—all she has to do is change her mind." Unlike me, Tori couldn't help thinking. This *is* my last chance.

Somebody knocked on the outer door. "Hello? Nancy Suhr here—Sports News Network. Is Tori Carsen in there?"

"It's a reporter!" Tori whispered.

Jill put her finger over her lips to signal Tori not to say a word.

"Tori can't talk right now!" Jill called to the reporter.

"But I'm the only official reporter allowed behind the scenes. Our viewers would love to see what it's like before a competition. . . ."

"Sorry. Tori's . . . getting changed right now," Jill told her.

"I'll wait," the reporter said.

Jill glanced at Tori and grinned.

After a minute, the reporter knocked on the door. "Well? Is she ready for an interview now?"

"Oh, gee. Sorry. She's washing her face," Jill said.

Tori put her hand over her mouth to keep from laughing out loud.

"Jill Wong? Is that you? I'd love an interview with you, too. And since you've already skated . . ."

"Sorry, I can't talk right now. I'm brushing my teeth," Jill said. "And after that I'll be flossing."

"Okay, okay," the reporter grumbled. "I get the point!"

"Um . . . we *might* have some time after we skate our long programs Friday," Jill suggested.

"Whatever," the reporter muttered. Tori pressed her ear against the door. She heard the reporter walk off.

"She's gone. Phew!" Tori giggled. "Jill, that was awesome."

"I didn't like it when I didn't get attention as an alternate," Jill said. "But I didn't know being on the team meant reporters even follow you into the bathroom!"

"Now you know," Tori said.

"Well, somebody should change the rules," Jill said. "No press allowed at the rink—ever."

"If cameras were banned from the rink, it would be a little hard for us to get our pictures in the paper and stuff," Tori pointed out.

"True." Jill brushed a wisp of damp black hair off her forehead. "But it might be worth it."

Tori groaned as her stomach turned over. "I don't even want my picture in the paper. Everyone's expecting me to fall, Jill. They know about my muscular dystrophy. They think it's only a matter of time before I collapse like I did at Nationals. And they all want to be there when it happens," Tori said bitterly.

"Tori, that's not true. Everyone's rooting for you!" Jill said. "You heard what Haley said. The whole country is behind you—behind *us.*"

Tori couldn't believe she had to perform after a Japanese skater. Even though the girl before her hadn't skated perfectly, she was the hometown favorite. Tori knew from experience that it was horrible to skate after somebody who had brought down the house.

I'll just have to make them forget about her, Tori told herself. She smoothed down the skirt of her seafoam green dress. Then she skated to center ice and struck her opening pose. The generous applause from the audience gave her a boost of confidence.

The first strains of Tori's short program music came through the speakers. It was a lively piece called "Gaite Parisienne," with one part that sounded as if cancan dancers should be skating along with Tori.

But from the opening notes, Tori could tell this wasn't going to be her night. Her legs felt weak and wobbly, and she had to concentrate twice as hard as usual to make her body do what she wanted it to. Instead of moving naturally, Tori felt as if she were forcing her muscles. She felt like a jerky robot.

She landed her double axel. Then she moved to the other end of the rink for her combination jump, a triple Lutz–double toe loop. She wobbled a little on the landing.

Concentrate, she told herself. The crowd reacted as if she were doing wonderfully. Tori relaxed a bit. She went into her spiral sequence. Her leg shook a little during her back spiral.

Tori moved into her spin combination. First the camel, then the sit spin, a back sit spin, and then she finished by grabbing her left foot behind her and pulling it high overhead.

Tori set up for her triple loop jump. She soared high, but she had to fight for the landing, struggling not to fall or to put her hand on the ice to catch her balance. Her legs wobbled from the strain. She nearly fell down, but somehow she managed to stay up. It had thrown off her timing, though. Suddenly she was a few beats behind the music, and her moves were out of sync.

Don't panic! she told herself. Just catch up!

The rest of her program went by in a blur. Tori did everything right, but she didn't feel good about it. She'd been so busy worrying about not falling, she hadn't put enough emotion into her skating. She knew the judges wouldn't like that.

The audience didn't seem to mind, though. They clapped ferociously, whistling and tossing gifts for Tori onto the ice. She waved politely at them, then skated off the ice and into Dan's waiting arms.

"Good job," he said, helping her over to the kiss-and-cry area.

"Good, but not great," Tori said, panting.

"Honey, you're exhausted," Mrs. Carsen said.

"Of course I am," Tori said. She picked up a bottle of mineral water and gulped some while she waited.

Her muscles were sore and tired—she'd barely made it off the ice.

Tori's scores came up. They were better than Jill's, but not by much. And she was definitely second to Tracy Wilkins, who had skated earlier.

"Excellent start. You're in good standing to make a move up. You'll catch Tracy on Friday," Dan told her.

Tori stood up and walked over to the boards to watch the next skater. Her right leg wobbled and she gripped the wall, steadying herself.

Jelena was on the ice. She was wearing an elegant, all black outfit. She looked beautiful and sophisticated.

"Come on, honey—sit over here with me," Mrs. Carsen urged. "Don't waste your energy standing."

Transfixed by the dramatic opening of Jelena's program, Tori let her mother guide her over to a chair. She winced as she sat down, feeling stiff. She had an excellent view of the ice. Dan walked over and stood near her.

Tori gasped as she saw Jelena's jump combination—the triple Lutz–double toe loop. Jelena looked as if she were flying through the same jumps Tori had struggled so hard with minutes earlier.

Watching the rest of Jelena's program made Tori feel worse and worse. Her muscles were hurting her. She couldn't jump very well *now*. And in a few more months . . . she probably wouldn't be able to jump at all.

"You'll be lucky if you're still walking." That's what

one of the doctors her mother had dragged her to told Tori a few weeks ago. The words haunted her as she watched Jelena move into a perfect series of spins. Jelena finished with a gorgeous flying camel.

Tori's whole body slumped as she waited for the final results of the short program. She felt as if she'd skated for two hours and forty minutes, instead of two minutes and forty seconds.

Finally the results flashed on the giant screen above the rink:

1. Tracy Wilkins USA
2. Jelena Cherkas RUS
3. Tori Carsen USA
4. Jill Wong USA

"Tori, you were great!" Natalia walked up behind her and squeezed her shoulder. "I am so proud of you and Jelena."

Tori didn't say anything. She didn't feel proud of herself.

"Tori, don't look so sad. You're in a great position going into the long program," Dan told her.

"Dan's right," Mrs. Carsen added. "Tracy had an awesome day, but she won't skate as well on Friday—she's not consistent. Forget about her—Jelena is your number-one competition."

"I know. And I'll never beat Jelena, Mom. Face it!" Tori snapped, rubbing her thigh muscles.

"Don't be ridiculous," Dan said. "You can beat her if you want to badly enough."

Tori glared at him. Even Dan, the best coach she'd ever had, didn't understand how badly she wanted to win. If he did, he'd never say something like that.

"I do want to win," Tori said, getting to her feet. Her calf muscle cramped again, and she stumbled a little as she tried to walk away. "But it's not up to me anymore. It's up to this stupid disease!"

17
Jill

"**I** can't *stand* all this waiting." Jill drummed her fingernails against the table. "I wish we could just skate today and get it over with!"

It was Thursday, and Jill and Tori were having lunch with their mothers at the hotel restaurant. It was a cold, snowy day, so they'd decided to stay indoors.

"I know, honey, but you can't skate today. And in the meantime, you're so worked up that you haven't eaten a thing," Mrs. Wong said. She pointed at Jill's full plate of salad.

"I keep thinking about Cara. And how she moved all her junk out of our room. She's probably on a flight home right now." Jill's heart sank.

"You haven't eaten, either," Mrs. Carsen observed, watching Tori closely. "Are you feeling all right?"

Jill looked at her friend. Tori had dark circles under her eyes. She didn't look very healthy.

"I feel okay, but I can't eat," Tori said. "I spent all morning going over the results and trying to figure out what I'd need to move up from third place. I think I should get a medal just for all the *math* I've done."

Jill smiled. She was glad to see Tori joking around, even though she was obviously feeling worn out.

"Let's see. Tracy is in first place. Jelena's in second," Mrs. Carsen said, making some notes on her napkin. "Then you, Tori. Then Jill. In order for you to win—"

"Jelena has to come down with a stomach flu, or be deported," Tori finished.

Jill giggled.

"Tori!" Mrs. Carsen cried.

Tori shrugged. "It was just a joke."

"As much as I'd like her to lose, I think the only solution is that we have to nail our long programs," Jill said. She shrugged. "Same as always . . . *impossible* as always. Did you see all those cameras—at every angle around the rink?"

Tori nibbled on a cracker. "Dan taught me how to block them out. Which I can do, once my program starts. But before then . . . I thought I was going to get sick yesterday, from all the attention."

"I know. But remember—the pressure is affecting everyone else, too," Mrs. Wong reasoned.

"Exactly," Mrs. Carsen agreed. "So maybe everyone will skate a little less than perfectly tomorrow night. Not that I want anyone to do badly. Of course I don't. But if Jill and Tori can sneak in there and grab a medal . . ."

"Mom, you're so competitive! Maybe you should be the one skating tomorrow night," Tori teased.

Mrs. Carsen smiled, looking embarrassed. "Sorry. I get a little carried away."

"No matter what happens, if both of you skate your best, I'll be very proud," Mrs. Wong said.

"And so will I." Mrs. Carsen put her hand over Tori's hand and then Jill's. "You've already done a great job, making it into the top five."

"Top five? I'm sorry, but that's just not good enough. I have my heart set on taking home the gold." Tori shot a straw wrapper across the table at Jill. "And I promise you can come visit it at my house, anytime you like."

"You know, Tori, there is such a thing as being *overly* confident," Mrs. Carsen warned. "But just this once, I'm willing to go along with it." She smiled.

Jill was glad to see Tori and her mother getting along so well. But Jill was afraid that Tori might not be able to win the gold. Her body seemed to be failing her more every day. Still, as long as they had a day to wait, and talk, and hope, anything was possible.

Jill woke up Friday morning and rolled over in bed. At least ten seconds passed before she realized what Friday meant. Friday . . . the long program . . . the Olympics!

Jill sat up, rubbing her shoulders. She must have been twisted up when she slept—her shoulders felt sore. She could barely raise one arm above her head.

"Great," she muttered, getting out of bed. She stared at her reflection in the mirror. There was a giant crease across her cheek from the pillow. "Double great."

There was a knock at the door. Jill went to answer it, hastily rubbing her cheek. "Who's there?"

"Jill? It's me," a soft voice replied. "Can I come in?"

Cara! What is she doing here? Jill thought.

"Of course you can come in. It's still your room," Jill said. She stepped back and opened the door wide. Then she turned around and went back to sit on her bed. She'd keep out of Cara's way for however long Cara stayed.

"Did you forget something?" Jill asked.

Cara hobbled into the room.

Sure she's ready to skate in the Olympics, Jill thought bitterly. She can hardly walk without limping!

"I did forget something," Cara said slowly, sitting on her old bed by the door. "I forgot to apologize."

Jill stared at her. "What?"

"I should have apologized to you yesterday. I know you have enough to think about without being mad at me, too," Cara said.

"Well . . ." Jill didn't know what to say. The last

thing she'd expected was for Cara to come back and apologize. "I thought you were already on your way home."

"And miss the rest of the Games? No way," Cara said. "I mean, it's going to be really hard for me to watch you skate tonight, Jill. *Really* hard. I didn't see any of Wednesday's short program—I had to get out of there."

Jill nodded. "I understand."

"Do you?" Cara asked in a loud voice.

"Well, I'm trying," Jill said defensively. "Help me."

Cara shook her head. "Sorry—I didn't mean that as angrily as it sounded. It's just that . . . this is my last Olympics, Jill. I'm going to college next year."

Jill waited while Cara wiped tears from her eyes.

"The other years, I wasn't ready for the Olympics. I wasn't a good enough skater. Now I am good enough, but it doesn't matter. I can barely walk, never mind skate." She sighed. "I just can't believe it has to end this way. I'll always be one of those skaters who won Nationals, but never an Olympic medal. Everyone forgets about those skaters."

"No, they don't," Jill said.

Cara shrugged. "Maybe. But I'm still having a really hard time accepting that this is the end for me. And I'm sorry if you got mixed up in the middle of that."

"This doesn't have to be your last Olympics. You *could* come back and skate in Salt Lake."

"Against you? Forget it," Cara laughed. "You'll be four years better, and I'll be four years *older*."

"People have done it," Jill said. "Great skaters like Brian Boitano and Katarina Witt, to name a few."

"I don't plan on making a comeback just yet. But then, I didn't plan on quitting skating now, either." Cara sighed again. "Can you forgive me for acting like such a jerk? I know you didn't try to hurt me. We crashed—both of us. I just happened to land on my ankle, which was already about as strong as a wet noodle."

Jill felt a huge weight lift from her shoulders.

"A Japanese noodle? Or a lasagna noodle?" Jill teased.

"Forget about my stupid ankle! Will you forgive me or not?" Cara asked.

"Yes," Jill told her. She leaned over and hugged Cara tightly. "I'm so sorry about what happened. But I'm glad we got to be friends."

"Me too," Cara said. "Jill, I want you to know that I told Mrs. Vandervleet the accident wasn't your fault. I withdrew my complaint, too."

"Thanks," Jill said. She felt a hundred pounds lighter already.

"Now. About tonight." Cara smiled at Jill. "You've got to make sure you land all your triples."

"Duh," Jill said. "I know that!"

"Yes, but did you know that if you can hit your take-offs exactly right, you can add a whole inch to the jump's height? And with Jelena Cherkas jumping, you'll need every inch. And maybe you should do an extra triple. You know, throw it in while you're skating, maybe at the end of your program when you're supposed to be tired, so nobody will be expecting it. And then—*bam!* You totally impress the judges, and the crowd goes wild.''

"You make it sound so easy,'' Jill said with a laugh.

"That's because I know you can do it,'' Cara told her.

"Well, thanks for your support. And you know what? If I do win a medal, I'll be sure to thank *both* my coaches,'' she teased Cara.

Just two more jumps, Jill told herself, moving down the ice. She turned, focusing on her right foot as she approached the jump. She took off with her left foot, punching straight up and turning three times before she landed. She held the landing with her arms outstretched, gliding smoothly down the ice. The crowd roared with applause.

Just one more jump, Jill told herself. She lifted into the air, completing a triple flip with no difficulty. Then she skated to center ice, went into a combination spin, and finished with her arms above her head, spinning at top speed.

The applause was deafening. Jill bowed to the audience, first to one side of the rink, and then to the other. She waved a few times and skated off the ice.

"You were terrific!'' Ludmila cried, enveloping Jill in her arms. "You were better than ever!''

"Thanks," Jill said, brushing a tear off her face. She and Ludmila moved to the kiss-and-cry area. Jill grabbed a small towel and wiped the sweat off her face and the back of her neck.

Nancy Suhr, the reporter for Sports News Network, was waiting behind Jill's chair.

"Can we talk *now*?" she asked Jill, who only nodded. She was too out of breath to speak. "How did you feel?" the reporter asked Jill.

"Great. No problems," Jill told her. She turned back around and watched the video screen anxiously, waiting for her scores to appear.

When they did, Jill nearly fell off her chair.

"Yes!" Ludmila cried when the first set of marks, for technical merit, came up.

"Five point eight, five point eight, five point nine . . . ," the announcer said, reading off each score.

Jill's heart started beating even faster. If her scores stayed this high, she might win a medal.

"Look at your scores for artistic merit!" Ludmila cried. "All five point eights! Congratulations, Jill. Look at the video screen up there—you're in first place."

"Not for long! Tori, Tracy, and Jelena haven't skated yet," Jill said.

Tracy Wilkins's name was called and she skated to center ice. She was all smiles as she began her program.

"She seems so relaxed," Jill said. "Like she's just out there to have fun."

Tracy launched into a triple salchow. She landed on the ice with an awkward thud, her feet in the air. The crowd groaned.

"It's okay, she'll recover," Jill said, watching as Tracy got up and skated back into her program. But she looked shaken. "Here comes her triple-double combination." Jill watched as Tracy attempted the first part, a triple toe loop. She only turned two and a quarter times before she came down, slipping on her edge and sliding into the boards.

The crowd let out a gasp.

"I feel so bad for her. She's better than that!" Jill said to Ludmila. "There's no way she can medal now."

"That's not good for the U.S. team, but it is good for you," Ludmila said as Tracy got to her feet to finish her program.

Jill watched as Tracy ended her program and skated off the ice. Next Jelena skated to center ice and her dramatic music floated out into the arena.

Jill watched Jelena land jump after jump with no errors. The Russian skater also conveyed the haunting, dramatic mood of the classical music to the audience. Jelena was jumping so well, Tori didn't stand a chance, Jill thought.

To skate better than Jelena was skating that night, Tori would have to be at the top of her form. And she wasn't anymore. Jill stared at the scoreboard. Jelena's scores were as high as five-nine—she even received a six. Now Jelena was in first place and Jill was in second. Tori would need a perfect program to win the gold. Could Tori still skate a flawless program with her weakened muscles? Jill doubted it in her mind, but she hoped so in her heart.

Then another thought occurred to her. If Tori did beat Jelena, then Jill would fall from second to third. With a shudder, Jill realized that she didn't know which she wanted more—the gold medal for Tori or the silver medal for herself.

18
Tori

Tori stepped out onto the ice, circling the rink as she warmed up. Flowers were still raining onto the ice for Jelena. She was sitting in the kiss-and-cry area.

Tori carefully stepped around a bouquet of red roses, narrowly missing the thorny stems. That was the last thing she needed right now—to fall on Jelena's flowers. She pictured herself tripping and breaking her leg. Her picture would be flashed across TV screens around the world, all right—as the world's biggest klutz!

The idea was so funny, it made a smile come to Tori's lips. And that made her relax enough to remember that she was here to have fun as well as to win. She loved skating. She wanted the whole world to know how much. Now was her chance to show them. Her last chance.

Jelena's scores were very, very good. But they weren't perfect. The door *was* open. Tori could win—if she skated cleanly.

I haven't been flawless lately, she thought. But I'm going to give it everything I have. What Jill had told her before the short program flashed through her mind. Jill had said she had nothing to lose. But Tori suddenly realized that she was the one who had nothing to lose.

This was her last Olympics. She might as well try to give the performance of her life. If she crashed and burned, fine—at least she would have given it her best shot, by skating at an even higher level than ever. She didn't know if she could do it, but the only way to find out was to try.

Taking a deep breath to calm herself, Tori skated over to her coach for his last-minute instructions.

"How do you feel? Are you ready?" Dan asked, smiling.

Tori nodded. She fingered the rhinestones around the neck of her white skating dress. Her mother had designed it, just as she had all of Tori's dresses throughout her skating career. The career that was almost over, Tori thought.

"Good. Now, remember—eye contact. And keep smiling," Dan said. He brushed a small speck of fuzz from Tori's cheek.

Tori nodded.

"Really stick that takeoff on your triple toe combination," Dan said. "Don't hold back. You've got to show the judges you're powerful."

Tori nodded again. She smoothed her hair, which was gathered back in a white clip made of the same fabric as her dress.

"This is it, Tori. You can do it. I know that, and everyone else here knows that too. So go show them!"

The announcer's voice boomed through the loudspeaker. "And now, competing for the United States, Tori Carsen!"

Dan pumped his fist in the air. "Go, Tori!" he yelled. The crowd erupted in loud whistles and cheers of support.

Tori's face broke into a wide smile as she skated to center ice. She lifted her arms above her head, striking her opening pose. She had only a second's wait, and then the music for her program began. It was set to balletic music from the opera *Faust*. Tori pushed off with her right leg.

Don't fall. Don't slip, she told herself. Nail your approach. She opened with a double axel, landed it cleanly, then curved in a pattern of steps down the length of the rink. She completed a triple Lutz. The next tough move was her first triple-triple combination. She moved carefully into a forward inside spiral, then did alternating Mohawks. Finally she stroked into her back crossovers.

Here it comes, she told herself. If she landed the first triple-triple, she'd know she was strong enough to make it through the program. She had to nail the jumps. It was the only thing that would make her beat Jelena.

She punched the ice with her toepick and took off into her triple toe loop. She landed cleanly, but she didn't even have time to notice. She was back in the air immediately, turning in her second triple loop. When she landed, gliding backward, the crowd roared with applause.

Suddenly, as she went into her combination spin, Tori realized she wasn't worrying about the mechanics anymore. She was just skating. For the love of it. It didn't matter whether this was for the first time or the last time. The fact that her muscles felt weak wasn't going to get in her way—not tonight.

Next she landed her triple salchow. Without thinking about it, her body was doing everything exactly the way Tori had trained it. She went into her second triple-triple combination fearlessly.

She hit her first triple toe loop perfectly and made her second one just as high and tight. When she came down, Tori heard the audience cheer. She smiled, doing a joyful hop as she turned to head down the ice, doing tricky, intricate footwork. The crowd loved that, too. As Tori finished her program with a split jump and then a stag leap, she realized they were on their feet, cheering and clapping. It was a standing ovation!

Tori struck her final pose and listened to the applause burst over the ice. Tori's body shook with emotion. She was almost afraid to move.

"U-S-A!" the crowd chanted. *"Tori, Tori!"*

Tori felt a lump in her throat. A tear trickled down her cheek as she waved at the audience. She curtsied toward one end of the arena and then turned to face the other end—and then both sides. Stuffed animals and bouquets of flowers were being tossed onto the ice.

Tori wanted to stay out there forever. She stood still, trying not to sob. The crowd grew even louder. Tori put her face in her hands.

It was over.

She had skated her best. And it had been incredible.

Tori looked up. U.S. flags were flying all over the stadium. She waved once more. Then she skated to the boards. Her fan club was waiting for her near the kiss-and-cry area: her family, Natalia, Jill, and even Cara.

"How do you think I did?" Tori asked, panting and out of breath as she stepped off the ice into Dan's waiting arms.

"Terrific," Dan said, squeezing Tori in a tight hug. "How did it feel?"

"Great," Tori said. "Like the best program I've ever done. Everything went exactly like it was supposed to. It was as if my body had memorized every jump and turn."

"You went up so high on that triple toe—I think you could have made it a quad," Dan said, kissing her cheek. "But we'll work on that. I mean, uh—sorry. Force of habit."

"No, it's okay." Still, Tori took a step away from him. As nice as that sounded, it simply wasn't going to happen. Ever. She wouldn't have the chance to work on landing a quad. This was her final competition. There wouldn't *be* any more training with Dan.

But now wasn't the time to focus on that. Now was the time to enjoy the moment, while she still could.

Tori sat down in the chair reserved for skaters, and Dan sat beside her while they awaited her scores. He reached over and squeezed her hand, as if to apologize for his remark a few seconds ago.

"Here it comes," Tori said softly. "The moment of truth."

"The truth, Tori? That's one of the cleanest and most exciting programs I've ever seen," Dan said. "And you know, I'm an old man. I've seen a million performances."

Tori smiled at him. "You're not old."

"I feel old! When was my Olympics? Twenty years ago?" Dan shook his head. "Unbelievable."

Tori bounced her knees up and down. She knew they were just babbling, but she couldn't stand the waiting. "What's *taking* so long?" she asked.

"The judges must still be deciding." Dan squeezed her hand tighter. "That means it's close."

The crowd started clapping, slowly, in unison. They stomped their feet. They clapped faster and faster to protest the slow scoring process. Tori felt as if the whole crowd were behind her now. Come on, she thought.

Tori chewed her thumbnail and stared at the small screen, waiting for her scores to flash. What was the holdup? She'd been finished for nearly five minutes. This was unheard of!

"Do you think the computer went down?" she asked Dan nervously.

"No. I think it's human error," Dan said. He tapped his head. "Slow brains."

Tori smiled, relaxing for a moment. Then, suddenly, the crowd let out a giant, collective gasp. Tori stared at the scores from the eight judges flashing on the screen in front of her. "For technical merit," the announcer said, "five point eight, five point eight, five point seven, five point nine . . ."

Tori's heart sank. Her scores weren't going to be good enough to win. Jelena's triple jumps were higher and crisper, and she'd done more of them. She didn't have a chance of winning against someone like that.

"Looks like it's silver," Tori said to Dan, who was staring at the screen, transfixed.

"Not necessarily," Dan mumbled. "Hold on, hold on." He seemed to be calming himself as much as he was trying to calm Tori. "You're still very much in the running."

"For artistic merit . . . ," the announcer said. The second set of marks glowed on the screen.

Tori stared at the marks. She couldn't believe it. She had four perfect scores of six—and the rest were all five point nines!

The crowd roared with approval—and confusion— as the scores were read off. It wasn't clear *who* had won—Jelena and Tori were nearly tied!

"What does it mean?" Tori frantically asked Dan. "Did I—did she—"

"That's it!" Dan cried, leaping out of his chair. "Tori, you won the gold!"

"I won? Really?"

"Don't take my word for it—look!" Dan pointed at the giant scoreboard above. In glowing letters, it read:

1. Tori Carsen USA
2. Jelena Cherkas RUS
3. Jill Wong USA

"I won the gold!" Tori shrieked. Before she could even move from her chair, she was mobbed by her family and friends in a group hug.

"Tori, you were so great!" Jill yelled.

"So were you," Tori told her. "Jill, we did it! We *medaled*!"

"Well, duh," Veronica said, crying. "I only told you that you would from the beginning."

Tori hugged her stepsister tightly.

"Hey, Tori, remember your idea that I should write to Evan? I did. I faxed him from the hotel. And he called me! He said we could talk when I get home,"

Veronica said. "I know how much you love sticking your nose into other people's business and then fixing their problems. That makes you even happier than winning the Olympics, right?"

Tori laughed and wiped a tear off Veronica's cheek.

"You know what would make me happier than winning the Olympics?" Tori said.

Veronica raised her eyebrows.

"Nothing!" Tori shouted. "Nothing could make me happier!" She turned to Natalia. "I'm glad I won. I'm sorry Jelena couldn't win, too."

"So am I," Natalia said. "But silver is very, very good. I just talked to her, and she'll be okay."

Tori hugged Roger, and then her father. Finally she was face to face with her mother. The one person who'd believed in her skating from the very beginning, who'd driven her to practice every day, twice a day, designed all her skating dresses, listened to Tori complain about every bad practice she'd ever had . . . It was almost too much for Tori to bear.

"We did it, Mom," she said. "We really did it!" She hugged her mother and burst into sobs.

"No, Tori. *You* did it." Mrs. Carsen sniffled. "And I have never been so proud of you in my entire life!"

Half an hour later, Jill stepped onto the bronze-medal platform, and an Olympic official handed her a giant bouquet of flowers. Then he lifted a medal on a ribbon out of a box. Jill bent forward, and he placed it over her head. Jill kissed him on the cheek, then stood up straight and waved joyfully to the crowd, holding the medal for everyone to see.

Next, Jelena stepped onto the silver-medal platform. She received her medal with a bland expression and held the bouquet tightly against her chest. Jill reached over to shake her hand. Jelena shook it, but she didn't look happy to be there.

Uh oh, Tori thought. She's really upset.

But she couldn't worry about Jelena. It was time to receive her medal. Tori stepped onto the top level of the medal platform, and the crowd cheered even louder.

The official put the gold medal around her neck. "Congratulations, Tori. We couldn't have a better champion." He kissed Tori's cheek.

"Thanks." Tori accepted the bouquet of flowers, then stood up straight, waving to the crowd. She waited a minute; then she turned to her right. "Congratulations, Jelena. I wish you the best. You're a wonderful skater."

Jelena looked up at her and nodded. She leaned forward to shake Tori's hand with a cold expression on her face. Then, without warning, she started crying. "You were the better skater tonight. You should win. *You* were wonderful, Tori."

"It's okay," Tori said, wrapping her arms around Jelena and hugging her close. "Don't cry."

"I'll try." Jelena brushed her tears away.

"Good. Now what I want to know is, when are you coming to Pennsylvania to visit us?" Tori asked.

"I will come soon," Jelena said. "Very soon, I promise."

"So, can a bronze-medal winner get a hug or what?" Jill asked, tugging on Tori's sleeve.

Tori turned around and hugged her friend. "Wait until everyone in Silver Blades gets a look at these, huh?" Tori clinked her gold medal against Jill's bronze medal.

"They can *look* all they want," Jill said. "But they can't touch. Right?"

"Well . . . for a fee, maybe." Tori laughed. "But no fingerprints."

"I guess Haley will be meeting us at the airport now," Jill said. "Because if I'm not mistaken, we're about to hear 'The Star-Spangled Banner.'" She stepped back onto the bronze-medal platform.

The music began to play, and Tori turned around to face the flag. She felt as if her heart were going to burst with happiness. As the flag was lifted higher and higher, Tori's eyes filled with tears.

Tori didn't know what her future held. But as she stood on the Olympic-medal platform—listening to the national anthem and gazing at the flag—she knew this was one of the happiest moments of her life. She would always remember it. And she would always have the gold.

Welcome to the 1998 Winter Games!

The crowds are roaring from the packed stands. The judges have taken their places. And your favorite figure skaters are waiting for their music to begin.

But what about you? Do you know what to look for as the champions skate, dance, jump, slide, and glide for the gold at the 1998 Winter Games?

This guide will help you follow the progress of your favorites in the figure-skating events.

Things to Do While You Watch the Olympics

1. Keep a notebook handy and write down all the interesting facts you learn about your favorite skater.
2. Write down the color of each skater's costume. At the end of all the events, you'll know which color is the season's hottest.
3. Fix your hair in a new style for your Olympic skating debut.
4. Look for commercials with no snow in them.
5. Predict the winners. Write down who you think will win gold, silver, and bronze medals in each event. When it's all over, check your predictions to see how many you got right.
6. Play "Name That Tune" with the program music. See how many songs you can identify before the announcers do.

7. Use paper and colored pencils to design your own skating costume.
8. Count how many skaters cry or hug their coaches after they get their scores.

Hot Trivia About a Cool Sport

- Ice dancing came to the Olympics in 1976. It's the newest figure-skating event.
- Judges watch the skaters practice their routines all week before the event. Some skaters even wear costumes to the practices.
- Thirty women compete in the short program for ladies' singles. Only the top twenty-four skaters move on to the long program. The remaining six may not finish competing in the Olympics.
- Judges are not allowed to look at instant replays. If they blink and miss a move, the judges have to guess to make their marks.
- Figure skating is the second most popular spectator sport in the country, according to the United States Figure Skating Association. The only sport more popular is NFL football.
- U.S. figure skaters have won more Olympic medals (thirty-eight as of 1996) than any other country's skaters.
- Precision figure skating is the fastest-growing skating sport. It's a team sport! Each team does a routine of fancy footwork, weaving lines, and synchronized movements.

The Olympics at a Glance

Ta-da! The opening flag ceremony is starting. The Winter Olympics are about to begin. There are seven sports and sixty-eight events, but the four figure-skating events are what *you've* really been waiting for. Understanding how each event works can be as hard as untangling knotted skate laces. Here's what's what:

The four figure-skating events are ladies' singles, men's singles, pairs skating, and ice dancing.

Thirty women, thirty men, twenty pairs, and twenty-four ice-dance teams from around the world will compete for four gold medals.

Singles skating for women and men means the skater performs alone. Singles skaters do two routines. First comes the short program; then comes the free skate program, also known as the long program. The skater who finishes highest in both phases of the competition wins the gold medal.

Short programs last two minutes and forty seconds. Judges look for style, strength, technique, and confidence. Each judge gives two marks to the performers. One mark is for technical performance. The other mark is for overall presentation, including style. The short program counts for one-third of the skater's total score. Both women and men must complete eight elements in their short program. These elements change from year to year, but generally include jumps, spins, and fast step sequences or fancy footwork.

Choose your favorite female skater and watch her

short program carefully. As she performs, check off the elements as she skates. Look for:

____ double axels
____ double or triple jumps
____ jump combinations (a triple jump followed by a double jump or two triple jumps)
____ flying spins
____ layback or sideways-leaning spins
____ spin combinations
____ step sequences
____ spiral step sequences

As you watch your favorite male skater perform, check off the elements as he skates. Look for:

____ double axels
____ triple jumps
____ jump combinations (a triple jump followed by a double jump or two triple jumps)
____ flying spins
____ camel spin or sit spins
____ spin combinations
____ different step sequences

The long program, or free skate, is four minutes long for women and four minutes and thirty seconds long for men. For this event, skaters are free to choose any moves and choreography they like. Judges want to see creativity, energy, and changes of pace. Skaters try to boost their scores by doing difficult, sometimes risky moves. Just as they do in the short program, skaters get two marks. One is for technical ability and one is for overall presentation.

The free skate program is the final event for singles skaters. Most fans like the ladies' free skate best. It's the last figure-skating event performed at the Olympics.

Pairs skating is for male and female partners. Together they perform difficult lifts and jumps. They mirror each other's moves and must have perfect timing. Even if they're skating on opposite sides of the rink, they must perform the same footwork and jumps. Pairs skating consists of a short and a long program, like singles skating.

The short program is two minutes and forty seconds long. It counts for one-third of the overall score. The short program has eight required elements. As you watch your favorite pair skate, look for:

_____ overhead lifts
_____ twist lifts
_____ side-by-side solo jumps
_____ spins
_____ step sequences
_____ spiral step sequences
_____ combined spins
_____ death spirals

The free skate program has no requirements. This gives each pair the chance to show off its best moves—which are usually the most *dangerous*! The death spiral, for example, requires the man to hold his partner's hands and spin in place while she twirls around him parallel to the ice. Yikes!

Ice dancing is truly dancing on ice. There are no required spins or jumps. Instead, a pair skates routines based on required dances. Skaters must avoid mirror skating, skating hand in hand, or skating one after the other. These moves would make the ice dancers look like pairs skaters.

Ice dancers must perform four routines: two compulsory dances, an original dance, and a free skate. The two compulsory dances come first. Each one is worth one-tenth of the total score.

In the compulsory dances, every pair performs the exact same dance to the same music. Skaters receive one mark for technique and one mark for timing and performance.

In the original dance, skaters are given a rhythm or type of dance, such as a tango or waltz. Their routine must be completely original. It counts for 30 percent of the total score. It's two minutes long, and skaters receive one mark for creativity and one for composition. In this dance, skaters must keep at least one foot on the ice at all times, except when jumping or lifting.

The free skate for ice dancing is worth half of the total score. It's four minutes long. Dancers choose their own music and create an original routine. Skaters are allowed to separate from each other only five times, for a total of five seconds. Skaters can use small lifts and jumps along with their fancy footwork. And, of course, they must be dancing!

Know the Score

Hey! What happened to the idea of 100 being the perfect score? Or 10? Most people are used to those numbers, so it may seem strange to see skaters jumping up and down when they get a score of 5.8. In figure skating, 6.0 is a perfect score. After completing an event, skaters' marks can look like this:

	AUSTRIA		JAPAN		U.K.		GERMANY	
	T.P.	A.I.	T.P.	A.I.	T.P.	A.I.	T.P.	A.I.
Smith	5.8	5.9	5.9	5.9	5.7	5.8	5.4	5.5
Jones	5.7	5.7	5.7	5.6	5.6	5.6	5.5	5.5
Adams	5.6	5.7	5.4	5.5	5.5	5.4	5.6	5.7

After the skaters have performed their routines, the scores for technical performance and artistic interpretation are combined and compared. Based on their scores, the skaters are ranked 1, 2, 3, and so on, depending on how many athletes are competing. In this example there are three skaters. So the highest rank is 1 and the lowest is 3. The German judge gave Adams a score of 5.6 for technical performance and 5.7 for artistic interpretation. That's the highest score the German judge gave. So this means Adams gets a 1 from the German judge. But Adams only gets 3s from the other judges, so she will not be in first place. Smith gets 1s from three judges. So Smith wins first place. In a real competition, when twenty-four skaters are being ranked by nine judges, this can get very complicated!

For the short program, there are mandatory deductions for certain types of errors. For the free skate, judges are given guidelines for scoring when a skater falls or lands a jump incorrectly. But they are only guidelines. Judges can give any score they want within the guidelines. For example, if a skater lands a double axel incorrectly, a judge can deduct anywhere from .1 to .4 of a point!

You Rate the Skaters

Now it's your turn—you be the judge! Fill in the blanks:

The best female skater was: _____

The best male skater was: _____

The best pairs skaters were: _____

_____

The best ice dancers were: _____

_____

The best costume was worn by: _____

The worst costume was worn by: _____

The best music was: _____

The best double jump was done by: _____

The best triple jump was done by: _____

The most dangerous-looking move was done by: ____

_____

The most graceful skater was: _____

The skater who messed up the worst was: _____

_____

The most popular skater was: _____

The skater who showed the most sportsmanship when the scores were announced was: _____

_____

The skater who behaved the worst when the scores were announced was: _____

The pairs skaters with the most interesting choreography were: _____

_____

The skater with the most playful routine was: _____

_____

The skaters I hope to see in the 2002 Winter Olympics in Salt Lake City are:

_____

_____

_____

_____

DO YOU HAVE A YOUNGER BROTHER OR SISTER?

Maybe he or she would like to meet Jill Wong's little sister Randi and her friends in the exciting new series

SILVER BLADES®
FIGURE EIGHTS

Look for these titles at your bookstore or library:

ICE DREAMS
STAR FOR A DAY
THE BEST ICE SHOW EVER!
BOSSY ANNA
DOUBLE BIRTHDAY TROUBLE
SPECIAL DELIVERY MESS
RANDI'S MISSING SKATES
MY WORST FRIEND, WOODY
RANDI'S PET SURPRISE
RANDI GOES FOR THE GOLD!

LEARN TO SKATE!

SKATE WITH U.S.
A SPECIAL PROGRAM FOR BEGINNERS

WHAT IS **SKATE WITH U.S.?**

Designed by the United States Figure Skating Association (USFSA) and sponsored by the United States Postal Service, Skate With U.S. is a beginning ice-skating program that is fun, challenging, and rewarding. Skaters of all ages are welcome!

HOW DO I JOIN **SKATE WITH U.S.?**

Skate With U.S. is offered at many rinks and clubs across the country. Contact your local rink or club to see if it offers the USFSA Basic Skills program. Or **call 1-800-269-0166** for more information about the Skate With U.S. program in your area.

WHAT DO I GET WHEN I JOIN **SKATE WITH U.S.?**

When you join Skate With U.S. through a club or a rink, you will be registered as an official USFSA Basic Skills Member, and you will receive:

- Official Basic Skills Membership Card
- Basic Skills Record Book with stickers
- Official Basic Skills member patch
- Year patch, denoting membership year
  And much, much more!

PLUS you may be eligible to participate in a "Compete With U.S." competition hosted by sponsoring clubs and rinks!

SKATE WITH U.S. *is an official program of*
THE UNITED STATES FIGURE SKATING ASSOCIATION

A FAN CLUB—JUST FOR YOU!

JOIN THE USA FIGURE SKATING INSIDE TICKET FAN CLUB!

As a member of this special skating fan club, you get:

- **Six issues of SKATING MAGAZINE!**
  For the inside edge on what's happening on and off the ice!

- **Your very own copy of MAGIC MEMORIES ON ICE!**
  A 90-minute video produced by ABC Sports featuring the world's greatest skaters!

- **An Official USA FIGURE SKATING TEAM Pin!**
  Available only to Inside Ticket Fan Club members!

- **A limited-edition photo of the U.S. World Figure Skating Team!**
  Available only to Inside Ticket Fan Club members!

- **The Official USA FIGURE SKATING INSIDE TICKET Membership Card!** For special discounts on USA Figure Skating collectibles and memorabilia!

To join the USA FIGURE SKATING INSIDE TICKET Fan Club, fill out the form below and send it with $24.95, plus $3.95 for shipping and handling (U.S. funds only, please!), to:

> Sports Fan Network
> USA Figure Skating Inside Ticket
> P.O. Box 581
> Portland, Oregon 97207-0581

Or call the Sports Fan Network membership hotline at **1-800-363-8796!**

NAME:_____

ADDRESS:_____

CITY:_____**STATE:**_____**ZIP:**_____

**PHONE: (____)_____DATE OF BIRTH:_____